M        Fraser, Anthea

         Symbols at your
         door

| DATE DUE | | |
|---|---|---|
| JUN 5 1991 | DEC 1 3 1991 | |
| JUN 2 1 199 | AUG 3 0 1993 | |
| JUL 8 1991 | | |
| AUG 5 1991 | | |
| AUG 1 6 1991 | | |
| AUG 3 0 1990 | | |
| SEP 1 3 199 | | |
| OCT 5 199 | | |
| OCT 1 0 1991 | | |
| OCT 1 8 1991 | | |
| OCT 2 5 199 | | |
| NOV 1 3 199 | | |

*Symbols at Your Door*

*By Anthea Fraser*

ANTHEA FRASER

# Symbols at
# Your Door

A CRIME CLUB BOOK

DOUBLEDAY

*New York   London   Toronto   Sydney   Auckland*

A Crime Club Book

PUBLISHED BY DOUBLEDAY
a division of Bantam Doubleday Dell Publishing Group, Inc.
666 Fifth Avenue, New York, New York 10103

DOUBLEDAY and the portrayal of a man
with a gun are trademarks of Doubleday,
a division of Bantam Doubleday Dell
Publishing Group, Inc.

Library of Congress Cataloging-in-Publication Data
Fraser, Anthea.
    Symbols at your door / Anthea Fraser. — 1st ed. in the U.S.A.
      p.   cm.
    "A Crime Club book."
      I. Title.
    PR6056.R286S96   1991
    823'.914—dc20                                          90-49974
                                                              CIP

ISBN 0-385-41685-7
Copyright © 1990 by Anthea Fraser
All Rights Reserved
Printed in the United States of America
May 1991
10  9  8  7  6  5  4  3  2  1
First Edition in the United States of America

*Symbols at Your Door*

# GREEN GROW THE RUSHES-O

I'll sing you one-O!
(*Chorus*) Green grow the rushes-O!
  What is your one-O?
One is one and all alone and evermore shall be so.

I'll sing you two-O!
(*Chorus*) Green grow the rushes-O!
  What are your two-O?
Two, two, the lily-white Boys, clothed all in green-O,
(*Chorus*) One is one and all alone and evermore shall
  be so.

I'll sing you three-O!
(*Chorus*) Green grow the rushes-O!
  What are your three-O?
Three, three the Rivals,
(*Chorus*) Two, two, the lily-white Boys, clothed all in
  green-O,
One is one and all alone and evermore shall be so.

Four for the Gospel-makers.
Five for the Symbols at your door.
Six for the six proud Walkers.
Seven for the seven Stars in the sky.
Eight for the April Rainers.
Nine for the nine bright Shiners.
Ten for the ten Commandments.
Eleven for the Eleven that went up to heaven.
Twelve for the twelve Apostles.

*Some of the residents of Beckworth*

At Beckworth House: the Duke and Duchess of Hampshire

At the Lodge: Neil and Alison Carey and daughter Philippa

At Coppins Farmhouse: Stewart and Carol Dexter and children Jenny and James

At Mews Grange: Bob and Gina Cummings, her mother Edith Irving, and sons Andrew and Duncan

At No. 1 Old Schoolhouse: Leslie and Joyce Scott

At No. 2 Old Schoolhouse: Giles and Lalage Parrish

At the Green Man: Stan and Doris Haydock

At No. 17 Tinker's Lane: Joe and Hazel Barlow, Joe's father Bert, daughter Mavis and son-in-law Lenny Hobbs

# CHAPTER 1

Stewart Dexter put his head round the kitchen door, his face tight with anger. "Which of you two has been scribbling on the front door?" he demanded furiously. The children seated at the breakfast bar looked up at him blankly.

"Come on, I intend to find out, and until the culprit owns up there's no pocket-money for either of you. Or were you both in on it?"

Carol, glancing at the children's bewildered faces, said quietly, "Just a minute, Stewart. What exactly are you talking about?"

"A bloody great scrawl in green felt-tip, that's what I'm talking about. What the hell got into you?" He glared at his son and daughter, whose uncertainty had given way to indignation.

"It wasn't me!" declared nine-year-old Jenny, adding virtuously, "I don't go scribbling on doors!"

"Nor do I!" James said hastily.

"I suppose it was the fairies?"

"Look, Stewart, if the children say they didn't do it, then they didn't. Let's go and see what all the fuss is about."

Her husband stood aside for her, his anger still simmering, and the children slipped off their stools and followed them outside.

"Good heavens!" Carol exclaimed. The graffito was a large, crudely drawn face with its tongue sticking out, and unaccountably she shivered. Basic as the drawing was, emanating from the screwed-up eyes, the protruding tongue and spiralling curls was a definite sense of malevolence.

"Well?" Stewart demanded.

"We didn't do it, Daddy," Jenny said, sounding suddenly subdued. Perhaps the malice had touched her, too.

"It might have been the 'Beckworth Bruisers'," Carol hazarded, using the name Stewart had coined for the village youths. She'd seen a group of them last night, watching her and whispering together as she walked back from the pillar-box.

"Let me catch them at it, that's all." He looked at his watch. "I must go, or I'll miss the train. See you this evening." Kissing her hastily, he got into the car and drove out of the gateway.

Carol said, "Hurry and finish your breakfast while I wash this off. We must leave for school in ten minutes."

But though she was able to remove most of the scrawl, a faint outline remained and the shine had been lifted off the polish. Until the door was retouched, the shadow of the face would be discernible, and she was surprised how much this discomfited her.

It had been an unusually quiet month at Carrington Street Police Station, and DCI Webb, looking out of his window at the cloudless blue sky, promised himself a painting trip during the coming weekend. Easter was early this year, and the unseasonally mild weather a bonus not to be wasted. All that was on the books was a spate of burglaries in the affluent outskirts of north Shillingham, and Crombie was handling that. They'd probably call in the Regional Crime Squad, anyway, since suspicion was growing that a motorway gang was to blame; Shillingham lay within fifteen minutes' drive of the M4, and the thieves could count on being thirty miles away before the break-ins were discovered.

He glanced across at the inspector, bent over his files. "Any joy, Alan?"

"Not so far; in fact there's another in today. Same MO but in Beckworth, would you believe. Seems a remote little place, yet it's roughly the same distance north of the motorway as we are south."

"Won't please His Grace!" Webb said with a grin. The village of Beckworth, cradled in the Chantock Hills which bisected the county from north-west to south-east, owed its fame and its very existence to Beckworth House, the ancestral seat of the Dukes of Hampshire.

Oddly enough, Beckworth House had come up in conversation only yesterday, when Hannah'd told him Mark Templeton's wedding reception was to be held there. This weekend, at that.

Webb thought back five months to his own meeting with Templeton and his bride. As usual, he reflected wryly, it was murder that had occasioned it. Well, they were a nice enough young couple, and since they'd withstood the pressures that beset them at the outset of their relationship, they would probably survive. He wished them well.

He glanced at the clock on the wall and pushed back his chair. "Coming to the Brown Bear for a bite to eat?"

Alan Crombie took off his spectacles and rubbed his eyes. "Yes, I could do with a break. Your shout, is it?" he added slyly.

Webb grinned. "I'll toss you for it," he said.

Alison Carey stood at the window of her office gazing up the long, winding drive that led to the House. It was an idyllic outlook in the spring sunshine: primroses in the grass, a thrush diligently digging for worms—a scene as representative of the English countryside as any she could imagine. She hadn't realized, until the argument with Neil over breakfast, how much she'd come to love this place in the last three years. The sudden possibility of leaving it was a lead weight in her stomach.

It had hit her the harder since she'd woken that morning with a feeling of anticipation. Easter was only days away, and after Saturday's big wedding reception the House would begin its summer season, opening to the public on bank holidays, Wednesdays and weekends. Nor were the other days necessarily free; private parties were increasingly catered for, principally the growing number of tours whose members enjoyed dining with the High and Mighty —lunch at one Stately Home, tea at another, dinner at a third.

For along with other owners of historic houses, the Hampshires could no longer manage on takings from the dwindling number who paid their £2.50s to trail meekly down the drugget alongside the roped walkways. They had had to diversify, opening their doors in the winter months to art exhibitions, concerts and conferences, and sponsoring courses in country crafts such as lace-making and dried-flower arrangement.

But to Alison, the advent of the public queuing for tours of the house was one of the first signs of summer, and as such she welcomed it. It had been a shock, this morning, to hear Neil's very different views. Probably, she thought now, it was a throwback to his general resentment at his redundancy. But why should it surface now, when he was satisfactorily employed again? Whatever the reason, the argument had erupted without warning.

They'd been breakfasting in the tiny, sun-filled dining-room, and she'd made some laughing comment about breathing in as she squeezed past his chair. To her astonishment, he took her up on it. "You're right: we've no reason to stay in this doll's house, now I've a decent job again."

She'd stopped, coffee-pot in hand, and stared at him. "Neil, that was a joke! I love it here!"

"Oh come on, Alison; it's always been a tight squeeze. When we moved here we'd no option but to lump it. That doesn't apply any more."

He was serious, she thought, dismayed. "But Neil, it's home! And with Jonathan away, there's room enough for the three of us."

"You call this room enough? If I push my chair back, I scrape the wall. But the point, surely, is that you don't have to work now. Added to which, it's inconvenient my being so far from the office. I can't entertain clients at this distance, and even if I could, there's no way I'd bring anyone to this pokey little place."

"You were glad enough of it before," she'd retorted. "It was our salvation, a job for me with a house thrown in. You called it a gift from the gods."

"Yes, I was grateful, if you want to rake that up again. You kept us going and saw Philippa through college, while I sat around on my backside."

"You know I didn't mean that," she said quietly, her spurt of temper gone.

"But to put it bluntly, this is a tied cottage and I was never one for forelock-tugging and having to be grateful for the odd pheasant or hare passed our way. 'Yes, Your Grace, no, Your Grace, three bags full, Your Grace!' It sticks in my craw. And any minute now, the great yobbo invasion will start again and they'll all troop past our door and peer in our windows as if their miserable £2.50 entitled them to every last ounce of our privacy."

She'd gazed at him, appalled. This was the first time he'd voiced any misgivings, but the acrid fluency with which they'd been delivered seemed to indicate he'd been brooding over them for some time.

"But I love it here," she repeated. "Not only the house, but the job. It's challenging and full of interest, and I'm good at it. And it's not only me," she continued, placatingly now. "Pippa's settled in her new job and Jonathan's near enough to pop over whenever he feels like it. If we moved, we wouldn't see so much of him."

"For heaven's sake, Alison!" Neil had exclaimed irritably. "Philippa's job's nothing special, she can always get another; and we certainly can't rule our lives to suit Jonathan. Once he's through college he'll be off, without a backward glance."

"Which leaves us," she said, still holding the coffee-pot.

"Yes." He met her eyes. "I know you've enjoyed it here,

and I accept that we couldn't have managed without it, but it's time to move on. In the end, it comes down to whose job is more important, yours or mine."

"That's not fair," she said. Emotional blackmail was what she meant.

He pushed back his chair, bumped against the wall, and swore. Alison had the unworthy impression he'd done it on purpose. "Anyway, we've not time to discuss it now; if I don't make a move I'll hit the traffic build-up. What bliss it would be, not having an hour and a half's driving each end of the day."

Which was how it had been left, hanging like a cloud over her. Because despite the fact that Neil had been out of work most of the time they'd been here, she'd been happier in this tiny house than she had for years. Was it because she'd felt he needed her, even depended on her while he searched for work? Or because she had such satisfaction in her own job? Or—her muscles tensed—was it really because out here he was unlikely to meet anyone he might be attracted to? And might that—boredom with herself—be the real reason he wanted to move?

Pushing away the familiar pain, she turned resolutely to her desk. But it was no good. The spring sunshine beckoned, and she needed to shake off her depression. Abandoning the paperwork, she decided instead to look in at the greenhouses and discuss the wedding flowers with Hazel. Professional arrangers would be coming on Good Friday, bringing the more exotic blooms with them, but the specially requested spring flowers had been grown on the estate.

Pulling the front door shut behind her, she set off up the drive between the tall cedars, their branches smudged with the soft blue-grey of new growth. Paths led off at intervals to left and right marked "To the statuary" or "The maze" or "The folly". Then, round a final bend, the House itself came into view, and she paused as she always did to gaze at its magnificent proportions, its graceful windows and glowing stone. Must she really give up all this?

"The Duke of Hampshire in Broadshire?" Neil had said, when she'd first told him she'd been offered the post of booking manager at Beckworth House. "A bit off-course, isn't he?"

She'd shrugged. "Dukes don't live in their title counties, do they? Norfolk in Sussex, Devonshire in Derbyshire. It's par for the course." At that stage the job had seemed a lifeline, a necessity to keep them going while Neil endlessly applied for positions. She hadn't expected it to become so important to her that the thought of leaving was a physical pain.

With a sigh she turned away, cutting diagonally across the broad gravel sweep in the direction of the greenhouses. She could see Hazel through the glass as she approached, bent over some plants. And there, she chided herself, was someone with more serious problems than she had; a son who'd been in trouble with the law and a tiny house, already overcrowded, which would soon be called on to accommodate an expected grandchild.

Shrugging aside her own worries, she smiled brightly and pushed open the greenhouse door.

When they'd first come to Beckworth, Carol had been horrified to learn that the nearest private school was ten miles away. Even the village one had closed, and a bus took the local children to and from Lethbridge each day. However, attempts to include Jenny and James in their number had fallen on stony ground. "The service is only for state schools," she was told uncompromisingly.

Still, now that the weather'd improved, she'd been enjoying the forty-minute round trip, and as Stewart somewhat tactlessly pointed out, she hadn't much else to do. In the six months they'd lived here, she hadn't met anyone she could remotely consider a friend.

That morning, for reasons she didn't analyse, she was in

no hurry to return home, and spent some hours listlessly wandering round the shops. If only Sue were here! she thought, and before she could stop it, a wave of longing for the past engulfed her. Why had she ever agreed to Stewart's suggestion that they move to the country? But with city violence on the increase and rates escalating, the roses-round-the-door syndrome had seemed appealing, as, on their house-hunting trips, had Beckworth. It had been a challenge, too, to buy the old house and renovate it to their taste. Now, with luxury kitchen and two bathrooms, the previous owners would hardly have recognized it.

But as she swiftly discovered, Beckworth had its drawbacks too. Everyone at their end of the village seemed either to commute daily or use their houses as weekend or holiday homes. During the daytime, you could walk up and down the main road without ever catching sight of a soul. True, the vicar had called, but Carol was no churchgoer. Envisioning a life of whist drives and committee meetings, she'd refused to be drawn, and, sensing her reluctance, he and his wife had tactfully withdrawn.

Then there were "the Bruisers". She knew it was stupid to be so apprehensive about them; they were, after all, only boys in their late teens and early twenties, some of them still at school. So why did she feel threatened any time she had to pass them? And now it seemed they'd crept up the path and drawn that hideous face on the door. In heaven's name, why?

It was lunch-time when, unable to delay her return any longer, she arrived home; but despite the time-lapse she tensed as she drove in the gateway. All this because some louts had scribbled on her door! None the less, she averted her eyes from the dull patch of wood as she inserted her key, and, after making a cup of coffee, sat down and dialled Sue's number.

"Carol!" The well-remembered voice added to her homesickness. "How are things?"

"Pretty grim." She needn't pretend with Sue.

"Oh dear. You're still not settled?"

"Not really. Do you know, I never see a soul from the minute I get back from dropping the children till I set out to collect them again. Except on Tuesdays, when the milkman helps out in the garden."

"But you can't be the only person in the village!" Sue pointed out reasonably.

"It seems like it, believe me."

"What about your neighbours?"

"Apart from a few retired couples, they all disappear at the same time as Stewart every morning."

"And the village people?"

"They're involved with their own concerns. Even in the evenings, we only see the young bloods, and them we could do without. They scribbled on our door last night."

"Well, Beckworth hasn't the monopoly on yobs; we've got them here too, or had you forgotten?"

"But it's much more impersonal in London. Here, they know who you are and where you live. It's—creepy."

"Does Stewart know how you feel?"

"Oh, he just says I should make more effort. At what, he doesn't specify."

"Well, cheer up. School's breaking up any minute and you'll have the children home."

"As it happens I won't. Stewart's sister's invited them on a camping trip and I didn't like to say no." She laughed suddenly. "I *am* being a drag, aren't I? Sorry, Sue; I'm just lonely, I suppose."

"Tell you what, in a month or so I'll leave my lot to fend for themselves and come over for a few days. How about that?"

"That'd be great. I'll look forward to it."

She felt better already, she reflected as she left the phone. She'd been letting things get on top of her because she'd no one to talk to. Stewart was right, she should make more effort. Perhaps she'd approach that woman at the Lodge; though only seen from a distance, she'd looked pleasant. If she had even one friend here, things would seem very different.

Humming under her breath, she was on her way to get lunch when the doorbell rang. Instantly she froze. Apart from the vicar, no one had called in all the time she'd been here. The drawing very much in mind, she opened the door cautiously, ready to slam it again, and found herself facing a uniformed policeman.

"Just got back, have you?" he said cheerfully. "I came round earlier." Then, seeing her rigidity, he added quickly, "Nothing to worry about, ma'am. There's been a burglary next door, and I was wondering, like, if you'd seen or heard anything suspicious?"

"A burglary?" That was all she needed! Her new-found optimism evaporated. "When?"

"Well, you see, ma'am, that's the trouble: we don't rightly know. The family are normally only here weekends, but as it's school holidays Mrs. Cummings brought the two lads and her mother over. They arrived mid-morning and found the place ransacked. You'll know them, I suppose?"

"No," Carol said, and added, "I don't know *anyone*."

The policeman looked at her in surprise. "Just moved in, have you?"

"We've been here six months."

Long enough to meet your next-door neighbours, he'd have thought. "Well, I know it's tricky with no definite time to go on, but can you remember seeing anyone loitering around, like?"

"Only the local boys."

"Right, ma'am, we'll check them out. Sorry to have troubled you."

Slowly Carol closed the door, all her latent fears resurrected. Suppose the burglary had taken place in the daytime? The thieves might think *all* the houses this end were empty during working hours. In which case they might try to break in here.

As the thought came she ran into the kitchen and tried

the back door. She'd locked it before going out, and it was still locked. She was being silly again. Standing in the middle of the room, she counted slowly to ten, by which time her breath had steadied. Then, though her appetite had now gone, she started to break some eggs into a bowl.

By mid-afternoon news of the burglary was all round the village. Edith Irving stood at her bedroom window, reflecting irritably that she'd seen more people pass the house in the last hour than she'd realized lived in the entire village. They'd come in ones and twos, walking with assumed nonchalance and casting swift, sideways glances at the house. Occasionally one of them caught her eye—after all, her window was only just above road level—and looked hurriedly away.

She craned forward as the fingerprint men's car emerged from the drive and turned in the direction of Shillingham. At least they had the house to themselves at last; now perhaps some attempt could be made to clear up. It really was too bad that Bob wasn't here. His place was with his family at such a time, not cooped up in an idiotic board meeting, though Gina wouldn't accept that.

"Come on, Mother, what could he do that we haven't done?" she'd asked in that infuriatingly reasonable tone she frequently adopted.

"He could at least lend some moral support. I don't fancy sleeping here tonight, I can tell you."

"It'll be the safest place in the village. Nothing to come back for, is there?"

Edith ignored her facetiousness. "Did you wash that scrawl off the door?"

"The boys did, while we were waiting for the police."

"And what had they to say about it?"

Gina'd looked at her in surprise. "The police? I never thought of mentioning it. It was only the local children, after all."

Which Edith could well believe. A scruffier bunch she'd

never seen. She supposed they could be thankful to be
spared obscenities, though the leering face had been unpleasant enough.

She sighed, staring discontentedly into the front garden.
She'd not wanted to come to this dreary place. For the life
of her she couldn't imagine what had prompted Bob and
Gina to buy it. Second homes might be a status symbol, but
they should be in acceptable places, preferably abroad. And
as far as the boys were concerned, there was much more to
do during the holidays at home in Richmond, as she'd
pointed out more than once during the past week. But she'd
been overruled as usual. She really did think they might
consider her wishes sometimes. As it was, Bob had merely
said, "No need for you to come, Ma. Stay here if you'd
prefer it." But he'd known she wouldn't. She was too nervous to stay in the house alone.

The telephone shrilled downstairs. Edith moved to the
door and, inching it open, stood listening. Bob, duly re-
leased from the board meeting, was returning Gina's call.

"No, darling, of course not," she heard her daughter
say. "There's no need, we can cope perfectly well. We'll see
you tomorrow evening as planned . . . Through the util-
ity room. It seems a professional job, the police say. Apparently there've been several in Shillingham . . . Well, you
can fix it over the weekend, but as I said to Mother, nobody's likely to come back tonight, are they? No, really, I'm
not nervous. Anyway, Kip would bark at the slightest
noise."

With a tut of annoyance, Edith softly closed the door
and looked round the room. Since she wasn't so foolish as
to leave personal things in this godforsaken place, nothing
of her own had been taken. The dressing-table drawers
were pulled open, and the fitted wardrobe, but the thieves
had found nothing. Even so, she proposed to wipe over all
the drawers and surfaces with disinfectant before unpack-
ing her suitcase. She hoped there was some under the sink,

because she didn't want to ask Gina for it. She'd only be accused of making a fuss.

It would have been so much more satisfactory, she thought for the hundredth time, if she could have made her home with Roy when Frank died. She'd always felt closer to him than to Gina, but that wife of his stood in the way. Roy'd been too loyal to say so, but Edith knew well enough why the invitation hadn't been forthcoming. Still, at least she was spared the indignity of being shuffled from one of them to the other, like an unwanted parcel.

There was a tap on the door and her elder grandson's face peered round it. "I've a bucket of water here, Gran, with some Dettol in it. Would you like me to give the room a once-over?"

"Bless you, Andrew, I'd be most grateful. How kind of you to think of it."

"Actually it was Mum. She knew you wouldn't feel happy till everything was wiped over." He set the bucket down and bent to wring out the cloth.

A mental apology to her daughter was in order, but Edith bypassed it. "Do we know yet how much they got away with?"

"We haven't finished checking, but the main things are the telly, the microwave and Duncan's old cassette player. He brought it up at half-term. Luckily I took my camera home last time we were here. It could have been a lot worse."

With which sentiment, if they'd had to have a burglary at all, his grandmother felt she could agree.

# CHAPTER 2

Hazel Barlow learned of the burglary from her father-in-law on her return from the greenhouses. Crippled for the last thirty years, the old man took a passionate interest in the village and its affairs, and was a familiar figure whizzing up and down the street in what Joe called his souped-up wheelchair.

"Proper carry-on there's been," he informed her, propelling himself after her into the kitchen. "Police knocking on doors asking questions. Even came here, wanting to know who lived here, and if we'd seen anything."

Hazel's instinctive reaction, swiftly suppressed, had been a shaft of fear. Could Darren be involved? Since he'd been in Shillingham he'd got in with a bad crowd. "Which house was burgled?" she asked, trying to sound casual.

"The old stables, though they've got some fancy name for it."

"Mews Grange," Hazel supplied, her mind still on her son.

He snorted derisively. "If they only knew it, I've spent more hours mucking out their precious "Mews Grange" than they've had hot dinners!" He watched as she poured boiling water into the thick brown teapot. "How are things up at the House? Ready for the opening?"

"There's the wedding first, but once that's over they'll be putting the kiosk up." She glanced at him affectionately. Despite his frequent awkwardness and bad temper, she was fond of him. "All set for Easter Monday?" It was the old man's duty, fiercely defended, to take the admission money and issue tickets.

"Well, I was going to Buckingham Palace, but I reckon I could put them off!"

"Get away with you!"

Joe Barlow came in the back door, removing his boots on the mat and slipping his feet into the carpet slippers that awaited him. Tall and broad-shouldered, he had pepper-and-salt hair and a countryman's reddened cheeks.

"Dad says there's been a burglary," Hazel blurted out, receiving a frustrated glare from the old man, whose news it was. But his son had already heard.

"Yep, one of the incomers on the top road." He washed his hands at the sink.

"Is it one you've been helping out?"

"I've been a couple of times, yes." A milkman by trade, Joe spent his free afternoons gardening, principally at Beckworth House but occasionally, by urgent request, at the newly renovated houses, whose owners didn't spend enough time there to keep their gardens in order.

He seated himself at the table and his wife pushed a mug of tea towards him. "Was much taken?" she asked.

"Nothing that can't be replaced." He shook his head humorously. "It beats me; they come here to get away from it all, and bring their tellies and stereos with them!"

"But have the police any idea who did it?"

He looked up at the note in her voice, and his face softened. "Professional job, they're saying. Been a couple of similar ones down Shillingham way."

Hazel closed her eyes on a wave of relief. At least that was one thing less to worry about. If she'd had to fear for Darren as well as fret about Mavis and Lenny and the baby, it would be more than she could cope with.

And the problem with Mavis couldn't be so quickly solved. When she and Lenny had married two years ago, they'd intended to buy their own cottage. But Beckworth, like many other villages, was now a desirable area for second homes, and property prices had soared beyond the reach of local people. Consequently, instead of Mavis moving out after the wedding, Lenny had moved in with them, and what with the front room given over to Dad, space was at a premium. Admittedly the young couple's wages helped the budget, but now Mavis was six months gone and about to give up work.

Joe had exploded when he'd heard, and it took a lot to rouse him. Irresponsible and selfish, he'd called it; they should have waited till they had a place of their own. At which Mavis had burst into tears and demanded when that was likely to be. But the baby, poor mite, would take up increasingly more space. As it was, Hazel doubted if a cot would fit into the small bedroom where Mavis had slept as a child and which she now shared with her husband.

"Hey!" She looked up as her husband's voice broke into her thoughts. "What do you have to do around here to get another cup of tea?"

She smiled quickly, reaching for the pot. "Sorry!" At least she had Joe, she thought thankfully, pouring his tea. With his matter-of-factness and plain common sense, he usually managed to calm her down. As though aware of her thoughts, he reached over and briefly laid his large, calloused hand over hers.

"Don't fret, mother-hen," he said. "We'll manage. We always have."

Detective-Sergeant Harry Sage stood outside the handsome oak door of Coppins Farmhouse and looked about him. "Pretty plush," he commented to DC "Fred" Perry. "Last time I drove through the village this was a real farm and the place we've just left, its stables. Been tarted up a bit, haven't they?"

"Amazing what money can do," Perry agreed. The house was sideways on to the road, a long, low building in honey-coloured stone. The old farmyard had been divided between the two houses, and on this side of the wall transformed into an attractive patio, which was screened from the road by a high fence. Herbs had been planted between the stones and tubs of bay trees, and fragrant magnolias

were dotted about. Against the wall was a built-in barbe-
cue.

A tall man with fair curly hair opened the door to them.
"Mr. Dexter? Sorry to disturb you, sir. Sergeant Sage
and Constable Perry, Shillingham CID."

"Yes?"

"We're making inquiries about the burglary next door."

"Again? My wife said someone called this afternoon."

"That's right, sir, the Lethbridge uniformed branch. But
several people weren't home so we're doing a follow-up. If
we could perhaps come in for a moment?"

"I can't tell you any more than my wife did." Not very
willingly, Stewart Dexter motioned them inside. This was
enough to upset Carol again, he thought resentfully.

The hall floor was polished wood, with a carved chest
doubling as hall table. The sound of a children's television
programme came from the room on the left. Dexter opened
the door on the right and gestured to them to enter. A
pretty, fair-haired woman turned swiftly from the fireplace
and Sage's eyes moved appreciatively over her. Not at all
bad. He went towards her with outstretched hand, which
she perforce took.

"Police?" she repeated, echoing her husband's introduc-
tion. "You're not in uniform."

"CID," Sage said smoothly. "My warrant card, ma'am.
We've taken over because there seems to be a tie-in with
some trouble on our patch."

Carol's eyes dropped from his hot, searching gaze.
"Well, I told the other man all I know."

Sage turned reluctantly back to Dexter. "You didn't notice anything untoward yourself, sir? With being fairly
close, I mean."

"No, I didn't. We respect each other's privacy here. In
fact, we know very little about the other residents."

"Ah, that's a pity. I was going to ask about your other
neighbours, Mr. and Mrs. Parrish. We've not been able to
contact them yet."

"I believe they run an advertising business in Bristol. Couple in their forties. Seem quite pleasant, from what I've seen of them."

Which added nothing to what they'd already learned.

"They're out all day, of course," Stewart Dexter added, "so they're no more likely to have seen anything than I am."

"We don't know what time the break-in took place," Sage reminded him. "It could have been evening or during the night."

"Sounds carry more at night."

"Quite."

There was a short pause, but Dexter had obviously nothing further to offer.

Sage turned back to his wife. She was standing at the window, which looked out on the patio. "Are you here during the day, ma'am?"

"Part of the time."

"Oh come on, Carol, most of it."

"All right, most of it." Her voice vibrated with strain. "Apart from taking the children to and from school, doing my shopping, going to the hairdresser and so on."

"So you'll know your neighbours better than your husband does?"

"No, they're never here."

Sage suppressed a sigh. Talk about isolationism. "Right, well we won't detain you any longer. Thanks for your help."

Not, he reflected disgustedly as he got into the car, that they *had* been much help. "They could all be deaf and blind," he said to Perry, "for all the notice they take of each other. I've never met such a self-centred mob. When I make my pile, Fred, remind me not to move out to somewhere like this. If you dropped dead in the street, they'd probably just step over you."

Which last remark he was later to remember.

After the policemen had gone, Carol went to the den to round up the children for bed. She would be glad when it was time to follow them. It had been a most unpleasant day; first the obscene drawing on the door, then news of the burglary and no fewer than two visits from the police. She had the illogical feeling that it marked a watershed, that after today their lives would never be the same.

Closing her eyes, she imagined herself back into their London house. The dining-room would be on her left and behind her the kitchen, not as luxurious as the one she now had, but full of memories of the children's babyhood. And beyond the front door was the wide, tree-lined avenue and, only three doors down, Sue and Raymond's home. How *happy* they'd all been there! she thought passionately. If only they'd never left!

She opened her eyes as the children brushed past her and obediently started up the stairs. Slowly she followed them, supervised their baths, heard their prayers. When she returned to the sitting-room, Stewart looked up from the television.

"All right?"

"They're in bed, yes."

"I meant you."

"I suppose so."

"It wasn't our house that was burgled, after all."

"Not this time."

"Come on, Carol, snap out of it. You never used to be so nervy."

"No. I'm sorry. I think I'll go up to bed myself. I've rather a headache."

"Suit yourself." He turned back to the television. She knew he was annoyed with her, obscurely resentful that she hadn't adapted to the new life he'd organized for them.

Their bedroom was at the end of the house, its window overlooking the main road through the village. On impulse she switched off the light and, drawing back the curtains, pushed up the sash and leaned out.

Immediately opposite, lit by the street-lamps, were the three retirement bungalows, their windows dark. On her left lay Mews Grange, empty last night, inhabited tonight, and on her right, the Old Schoolhouse. It was a community of a sort, she supposed, but she didn't feel part of it.

She turned from the window and prepared for bed. But tired though she was, sleep would not come. Tossing and turning, her brain played tricks with her, merging the face on the door with the detective's insolent, hot-eyed stare— to her heightened imagination equally menacing.

But she must eventually have slept, for when the disturbance startled her awake, Stewart was lying beside her. For a moment, dazed, she lay still, trying to identify the sounds from beyond the open window. Then she slipped from the bed and stumbled across the dark room. The noise was coming nearer, individual shouts and cries now discernible, and the ominous sound of breaking glass. As she reached the window, she was in time to see a group of youths come hurtling round the corner of Tinker's Lane— from the pub, no doubt—and start running along the opposite pavement, pursued by a second group. A nervous light bloomed in one of the bungalows.

"What the hell's going on?" came Stewart's sleepy mutter. An extra loud yell brought him to join her at the window as one of the youths flung himself forward in a rugby tackle, bringing the boy in front of him crashing to the ground.

"The Bruisers strike again," Stewart commented. "I'd better go and sort them out." He turned back into the room, but Carol's fingers dug into his arm.

"*No!* Do you want a knife in your ribs?"

"Look, it's only a drunken brawl, but they'll wake the whole neighbourhood at this rate. If it was James out there, you'd be grateful if someone stopped them, wouldn't you?"

"But it isn't James," Carol said shakily, watching the bodies writhing on the pavement as late-comers flung themselves enthusiastically into the fray. "What's frightening is that there are no police for miles, probably no nearer than Lethbridge."

"Hey!" came an authoritative voice. "That's enough of that!" A tall, heavy figure strode purposefully into the mêlée and, seizing a struggling youth in each hand, dragged them clear.

"That's Joe, isn't it? The milkman?"

Carol nodded, watching with awe as he despatched the suddenly chastened pugilists.

"Well, good for him," Stewart said admiringly. "Perhaps we can now get some sleep."

But from a safe distance, the two gangs continued to hurl insults at each other. "Bloody gyppos!" jeered the village crowd. The retreating band spun furiously round, then, seeing Joe Barlow's implacable figure, hesitated.

"We'll come back when your nanny's not here!" they shouted back.

"*Are* they gypsies?" asked Carol, bewildered.

"I shouldn't think so; they're probably from the caravan park down the road. I saw several cars arriving there; for the Easter break, I suppose."

"Do you think they *will* come back?"

Gently but firmly, Stewart turned her from the window and propelled her towards the bed. "You'd do a lot better," he told her, "if you didn't waste your energies on worrying about what *might* happen but probably never will. Now go back to sleep, there's a good girl. It's all over now."

But his last words, far from reassuring her, struck a note of doom. It's all over now. That was precisely what she was afraid of.

Saturday morning, and still the fine weather held. Webb whistled as he slung his painting tackle into the car and backed out of the drive. It was still early and the roads wouldn't be busy for several hours yet.

Since Beckworth had been in his thoughts this week, he'd decided to drive in that direction. One of the highest villages in the county, it offered panoramic views and in winter acted as the local barometer, a harbinger of impending bad weather. "They say there was snow up in Beckworth last night."

As Alan had said, the village lay only fifteen minutes' drive from the motorway, at the centre of a triangle composed of Shillingham and Ashmartin to the south and Lethbridge at the apex. Nevertheless, because of its height it seemed remote, a place set apart.

Webb took the Lethbridge road out of town, between fields where the first lambs took unsteady steps under trees laden with blossom. Spring, spring, spring! he thought self-mockingly, but his spirits lifted none the less.

Alongside the sign for Beckworth, pointing to the right, was the stylized logo of a Stately Home, with the name Beckworth House beneath it. Webb turned into the narrow road which immediately began to climb, twisting and turning as it made its way into the forest that covered the hillside. Here and there the trees met overhead and dappled sunlight patterned the bonnet of the car. A board on his left read "Forestry Commission", another farther on exhorted horse-riders to keep to the bridle path. At regular intervals walkways led off into the trees, and he guessed that later in the day these empty lay-bys would be jammed with parked cars.

Gradually the trees retreated from the roadside and the view opened out. In his rear-view mirror Webb could see the land falling away behind him, the sheep and lambs mere blobs of white in the green fields. Round a corner he came suddenly on a caravan park, a hive of activity with cars and tents and children playing. Beyond the next bend was a lookout point, giving extensive views over the Broadshire Vale. He'd forgotten how lovely it was up here, and, at least at the moment, how peaceful. Later, he thought, the wedding cars would be following this same route, and he imagined Hannah already preparing for the ceremony.

The road was levelling off now, and farms began to line it. Then came the sign for Beckworth and he entered the village itself. The houses on his right seemed to have been done up since he was here last, double-glazing and high, neatly clipped hedges ensuring the privacy of their owners. He slowed down as he neared the crossroads, trying to get his bearings. On his right, a road led up to the church and vicarage as he remembered, but the school on the corner seemed to have been converted into private houses. He wondered what had happened to the children.

On his left, Tinker's Lane ran down the hill, keeping line with the high walls of the estate whose gates were immediately opposite. Webb could see the drive and some parkland through the ornamental scrolls, but the House itself, set well back, was screened by trees. And if he remembered correctly, the pub where he intended to lunch was just round the corner.

He turned into the lane and came upon it at once, the lettering on the wall identifying it as the Green Man. A young lad was brushing the forecourt, and Webb leaned out of the window. "All right if I park here for an hour or two? I'll be coming to you for lunch later."

"Don't see why not, mate," said the lad indifferently, which Webb took to be consent. He drove in and stopped in the shade of some trees which, with luck, would shield the car from the sun. Then, collecting his collapsible easel and paints, he set off up the road towards the church.

"You'd think someone would have heard something," Bob Cummings remarked. He was standing at the back of his house, fitting a piece of board into the frame of the broken window. It would have to do till after the weekend, when they could get the glass replaced. "I mean, the thieves must have had a van or something to shift the TV. Surely someone saw it being driven into the drive."

Gina watched as he hammered in a nail. "They'd probably assume it had a right to be here."

"Even if we weren't?"

She shrugged. "Does anyone know when we're here? More to the point, does anyone care? We haven't gone out of our way to make ourselves known, and the old people across the road don't strike me as particularly observant."

"There's the family next door."

"According to the police, they didn't see or hear anything." She glanced at the wall separating them from Coppins Farmhouse. "Perhaps we should make an effort to meet people, start a Neighbourhood Watch scheme or something."

"We couldn't contribute much, could we? Anyway, we don't really want to get involved, we've enough of a social life at home. The whole point of this place is that we can relax here."

"It leaves a nasty taste though. This seemed such a pleasant little village, so safe and sleepy. Why should anyone come all the way up here on the off-chance of a haul?"

"Search me. But unless it was one of the locals, which hasn't been ruled out, someone did."

"Gina? Are you out there? I've made a cup of coffee."

"Thank you, Mother," she called back, "we're just coming."

"Speaking of relaxing," Bob said, banging in the last nail, "it's a pity your mother won't. She puts a damper on everything, going round with that pained expression on her face."

"I suppose we must make allowances. She was really quite upset about the burglary."

"But she's the same every time we come, as though we forcibly drag her here against her will. Whereas I for one would be more than happy if she stayed at home."

"Hush," Gina said quickly, "she might hear you. I know she can be a trial, love, but she's old, after all."

"I just don't see why Roy and Vivian can't do a stint. It's all very well him being the blue-eyed boy, but he mightn't be quite so amenable if he had her twenty-four hours a day, three hundred and sixty-five days a year."

"At least," Gina said peaceably, "she'll keep house for the boys when we go to Greece."

"Not without reminding us for a month beforehand how lucky we are to have her."

Gina laughed and reached up to kiss his cheek. "I know it's hard sometimes, but bless you for putting up with it."

He slipped his arm round her, giving her a squeeze, and, arranging innocuous expressions on their faces, they walked round to the back door.

Webb laid down his brush and stretched. The sun was surprisingly hot and he was ready for a beer. From this vantage-point the village lay spread beneath him, and he was able to see over the high walls of the estate to Beckworth House, sitting placidly amid its beautiful grounds. And as he gazed down, he saw a white Rolls Royce turn into the now-open gates. The bride and groom had arrived for the reception.

It seemed only the bridal party was allowed to drive up to the House, since as Webb reached the road again, more and more cars were turning into Tinker's Lane and being directed into the large parking area under the estate walls. He was glad he'd left his own car in front of the pub, or he'd have had difficulty in extracting it. Men in morning suits and women in flimsy dresses and large hats were making their way, in small brightly coloured groups, up the winding drive towards the House.

Webb paused to see if he could discern Hannah among them, but without success. Just as well; he didn't want her thinking he'd come to watch the peepshow. Abandoning interest, he turned into the welcome cool of the public bar.

It was fairly crowded, but with drinkers rather than lunchers, and he guessed the majority of the clientele was local. However, a menu was chalked up on a blackboard.

He ordered a jumbo sausage along with his pint, and made his way to a vacant table by the window.

From here, he had a cornerwise view of the still-arriving wedding guests, but he was more interested in the immediate company. Farmers and estate workers in the main, he guessed. Such scraps of talk that he caught were of lambing and spring crops and the danger of a late frost.

The landlord, short and stout with rolled-up sleeves, brought over his lunch personally. "Passing through?" he inquired genially, obviously interested in a new face.

"No, I've been sketching up behind the church. What a lovely spot it is. I wouldn't mind living here myself."

"Ah, well." The landlord shook his head gloomily. "Things have changed a lot in the ten years I've been here. There's a different atmosphere nowadays."

"You mean the burglary?"

"Oh, you've heard about that? Yes, that's one thing. But the rot started long before, when Coppins Farm changed hands. Developers bought it, split the yard and converted the stables and cowsheds into another "desirable residence". They must have made a mint out of it."

"I see the school's gone, too."

"That's right, and the village shop-cum-post office. Tarted up and sold for a packet. The end result is that the locals can't afford to buy here any more. All the young people are leaving the village and soon we'll be no more than a holiday home for yuppies. The heart's gone out of the place, I can tell you."

"That's too bad," Webb murmured, eyeing his cooling sausage. "Can't anything be done?"

"Not as long as they can get £150,000 a time along the main road. Who hereabouts can afford that kind of money? Even the small cottages, which were ideal for a young couple, are now luxury retirement homes. Still, you don't want to hear all our troubles. Enjoy your meal."

He moved away and Webb turned to his lunch with a changed perception of the attractions of Beckworth.

# CHAPTER 3

Carol put her foot on the clutch and tried the ignition again. The engine gave a faint splutter and faded into silence. What was the matter with the thing? It had been perfectly all right yesterday. With decreasing hope she tried a third time, with similar results.

Her hands tightened on the steering-wheel and tears of frustration came into her eyes. What could she do? What would Stewart do? Get out and look under the bonnet? But she didn't know what to look *for*. Oh God, she *had* to get into Lethbridge this afternoon.

A tap on the window spun her round, to see a man smiling at her. "Need some help?"

"It won't start," she said.

"So I gathered. Have you flooded it?"

"Probably."

"Move over, and I'll have a go."

Obediently she slid across to the passenger seat and he climbed in beside her. This time a turn of the ignition brought no sound at all.

"I'm afraid the battery's flat," he told her.

"Oh *damn!* If only I'd tried it before my husband went out! He's taken the children for a walk and by the time they get back the shops will be shut."

"Where do you want to go?"

"Lethbridge. The children are going on a camping trip on Monday, and there are some last-minute things I need to buy."

"I'll take you," he said, surprising them both. Then, as her eyes widened, he added quickly, "Look, we're neighbours. I live over at the Lodge—Neil Carey."

"Carol Dexter. But I can't let you give up your Saturday afternoon."

"To be honest, I'd be glad of something to do. My wife's up at the House seeing to the wedding reception and I was feeling bored and neglected. A trip to Lethbridge would be a pleasure, I assure you."

He spoke no more than the truth; he'd spent the last half-hour moodily watching the guests arrive, resentful of Alison's absence. Admittedly there were plenty of things he could do but he couldn't settle to any of them. The main cause of his restlessness was the strained atmosphere of the last few days. But he'd been meaning to bring up the subject of their moving, and at the time it had seemed a good opportunity. Patently, it hadn't been; on the other hand, if Alison was as opposed to the idea as she'd seemed, perhaps there would never be a good time.

To fill in a few minutes, he had taken some letters to the pillar-box and then, strolling on up the road, had heard the spluttering engine. He was glad that he had; after the constraint of the last few days, a drive with a pretty woman would do him a power of good.

She was still protesting, and he cut her short. "Look, I'll go and get the car and meet you on the corner of the Lane in three minutes. OK?"

"Well, if you really are sure. It's very kind of you." She watched him walk back down the drive, tall and thin, with a light step. He was really rather attractive, with that crooked smile. Furthermore, apart from the vicar he was the first person in the village to approach her. Perhaps it would lead to a meeting with his nice-looking wife, and she'd have some friends here at last. At the very least, he'd come to her rescue now.

Stewart had been annoyed that she hadn't checked the children's things earlier, which was why he hadn't offered to take her to town. And he was right, she reflected, locking the useless car. She was usually meticulous about such things, but this week everything had been out of kilter and she hadn't been thinking straight.

Shopping-bag in hand, she walked down the road. The big gates stood open and she glanced up the drive expecting to see Mr. Carey's car. However, he emerged from the lane on her left and drew to a halt beside her, leaning across to open the passenger door.

"I was watching for you up the drive," she commented, as he made a U-turn and started back down the lane.

"No, we have a couple of the garages behind the pub. Saves having to open those heavy gates every time we go out." He negotiated a skein of cyclists. "How long have you been living here?"

"Six months now."

"And what do you think of our little corner of paradise?"

Perhaps it was the light sarcasm in his voice that emboldened her to say flatly, "I hate it." It was the first time she'd admitted the fact, even to herself, and she felt his surprise. Then he laughed.

"Well, well, welcome to the club! It's a very exclusive one; in fact I'd thought I was the only member."

She turned to look at him. "You don't like it either?"

"Like you, I hate it. Unfortunately, my wife doesn't."

"Nor does my husband. But it's all right for him; he's at work all day with plenty of company."

"So am I, now, but it hasn't changed my feelings. When we came here I'd just been made redundant, and it took over two years to find a job, during which I hung around here day after day. Even now, every evening when I come home I feel a creeping sense of depression. Association of ideas, I suppose."

"But your wife doesn't want to move?"

"No. She's very involved with her job, which she thoroughly enjoys."

"So what'll you do?"

"Grin and bear it, I suppose. At least for a while

longer." He glanced at her. "What do you dislike so much?"

"The loneliness. There's no one to speak to, no one even to *see* all day."

"We lead container lives nowadays, bound up in our own concerns. It doesn't make for neighbourliness."

"I suppose there's no chance of your wife needing any help?"

"I could ask her. There's a group of village women who bake cakes for the tea-shop at the House, but I imagine that's hardly your scene. Leave it with me anyway, and I'll have a word with her. Now, which car-park do you think we should make for?"

Up at Beckworth House, the wedding reception was proceeding smoothly. The meal was just finishing, after which a short break was scheduled before the speeches. Hoping to forestall the rush to the cloakroom, Alison made her way there. She was combing her hair when the door behind her swished open and a well-remembered voice exclaimed, "Alison! I didn't know you were here!"

It was Daphne Warrender, wife of one of the directors of Neil's previous company.

"Hello, Daphne," she said steadily.

"I didn't see you at the church. Where were you sitting?"

"I'm not a guest, I work here—as booking manager. How nice to see you."

"You *work* here? Well, good for you! Do you enjoy it?"

"Very much. We live at the Lodge and I organize all the events—fashion shows, dinner theatres, even the odd TV commercial. It's very interesting."

"You have Pippa with you?"

"Yes, she's secretary to a firm of solicitors in Shillingham."

"And Jonathan?"

"In his last year at agricultural college."

"Well, I think that's marvellous. I take my hat off to you." She opened her powder compact and bent forward to apply the puff. Her voice changed subtly. "Do you ever hear anything of Neil?"

Alison gazed blankly at her reflected face. "I beg your pardon?"

"I just wondered if you're ever in touch—through the children?"

Above the sudden clattering of her heart, Alison heard herself say, "Neil is personnel director of Banks Moorhouse, in Reading."

Daphne gave a low, malicious laugh. "Personnel again? Then no doubt he's up to his old tricks."

"I don't know what you mean," Alison said, more loudly than she could have wished.

Daphne's hand, applying lipstick now, suddenly stilled. In the mirror her eyes went to the other woman's stunned face. Then she slowly straightened and turned to face her. "Have I been speaking out of turn? Are you still together?"

"Yes." The single word was all she could manage, and she let it answer both questions.

"Alison, I am sorry. How clumsy of me. I just assumed that after all the scandal and his dismissal—" Her voice tailed off. She said quietly, "I'm probably making it worse. Please forgive my thoughtlessness. I think it's wonderful that you stood by him." She bent forward, patted Alison's resistant arm and, with a quick, bright smile, hurried from the room.

Round the bend of the L-shaped cloakroom, Gwen Rutherford and Hannah James, seated at adjacent dressing-tables, looked at each other with raised eyebrows. The unseen door opened and closed again. No one seemed to have entered so, assured that their unintentional eavesdropping would not be discovered, they rose and made their way back to the reception.

"That was somewhat embarrassing," Gwen commented

*sotto voce.* "I was praying they wouldn't come round the corner and see us."

"Yes; I imagine 'Neil', whoever he is, will have some explaining to do this evening."

Gwen Rutherford, as well as being the bridegroom's aunt, was headmistress of Ashbourne School for Girls, where he was a music master. Hannah, as her deputy and with no family obligation, had at first been undecided about accepting the wedding invitation. For the school, as well as being indirectly responsible for bringing bride and groom together, had also been involved in the tragedy which followed. But Mark and Gwen between them had swayed her, and she was glad she had come. It was a happy occasion, and no shadow from the past had been allowed to cloud it.

Idly, while Gwen spoke to her brother-in-law, Hannah thought of all the weddings she'd attended over the years, acknowledging that at some point during each ceremony she'd felt a fleeting stab of envy. Yet she could have married if she chose; she'd received several proposals in her time, though the only one she'd considered seriously had been the last, from Charles Frobisher less than two years ago. And in the end she'd decided against it. The reason she gave was her career, though as a governor of the school, Charles had had no objection to her continuing work. The real reason, as always, was David Webb. Ostensibly their relationship made no demands, since neither wished to marry or even to live together. But there was a commitment between them which neither wished to break, so they were only partially free. The ambivalent arrangement suited them perfectly, and Hannah acknowledged humbly how lucky she was.

The sound of a gavel broke into her musings, and she abandoned them and settled back to listen to the speeches.

With the meal over, Alison's self-imposed supervision was at an end. Mechanically she thanked both caterers and servers, congratulated them on the smoothness of the operation, and slipped out of the door into the sunny courtyard.

She had intended to go back to the Lodge and have a well-earned cup of tea with Neil. Then they could have attended to the box of bedding plants which she'd bought the other day. Now, however, she needed time before seeing him, time to assimilate what Daphne had hinted, and to examine her own reactions.

Accordingly, instead of walking back down the drive, she set off into the deserted gardens in the general direction of the lily-pond. Her immediate feeling, now she was free to assess it, was a mixture of hurt and anger. For Neil hadn't after all been made redundant; he'd been sacked, and Daphne's barbed comment left little doubt as to the reason.

Bitterly, Alison recalled her constant support at that time, her concern and encouragement as he searched more and more desperately for work. And all the time he'd been deceiving her, abusing her trust, and for all she knew continuing the association that had been his downfall.

She turned into the avenue of herbaceous borders which led to the pond. It was warm in this sheltered corner, the sun quite hot on her back. Reaching the pond, she sat down on the bench and stared out across the calm water carpeted with lily-pads. She had only two choices; to tell Neil of her meeting with Daphne, or not to mention it. Detachedly she considered each in turn. If she told him, it would almost certainly mean the end of their marriage. They had come close to divorce ten years ago over his involvement with another woman, but for the children's sakes—and, she reminded herself wryly, because she still loved him—she had agreed to stay with him. Now the children needn't be considered and, she thought suddenly, she herself was independent. The Lodge was hers for as long as she worked here, and she could support herself quite adequately.

And if she kept quiet? Life would continue as it had for

the last three years—unless Neil again brought up the question of moving. And that was the crux. Better, perhaps, not to precipitate trouble, but if he insisted on leaving Beckworth, he could go without her. Because should another crisis arise later, she would never again be in such a strong position.

Even as she reached her decision, she knew it would be difficult to keep her knowledge from him. Instinctively she wanted to lash out, to hurt him as, retrospectively, he had hurt her. But to do so would be counter-productive, forcing an issue which might possibly never have to be faced. And after all, the affair was now three years in the past. Perhaps, learning from his lesson, he had matured sufficiently not to stray again.

Across the gingham tablecloth Neil watched Carol Dexter's face as she talked. She was an attractive little thing, and she'd certainly brightened up his Saturday. Interesting, too, that she shared his disenchantment with Beckworth. Bored and lonely, she might well, he thought, respond to a little light-hearted dalliance, but he wasn't sure he'd bother to find out. He'd had the devil's own luck in keeping the last fiasco from Alison; it would be asking for trouble to become even casually involved with someone so near home.

"Did you hear the commotion the other night?" she was saying, helping herself to the last scone. "I thought we were going to have a full-scale fight on our doorstep."

"Not literally on your doorstep, I hope," Neil smiled, holding out his cup for a refill.

"On the pavement opposite, actually. But they *have* been on our doorstep, or someone has. A revolting face was drawn on the door, and though I've scrubbed at it several times, I can't get rid of it." She gave an involuntary shudder.

"I shouldn't let it worry you," he said, surprised at the violence of her reaction. "We were treated to one, too."

She stared at him. "Someone drew on your door?"

"That's right; a face with its tongue out. Charming, isn't it? And it's not as if the House had been open; you get all sorts of weirdos then."

"When did you discover it?"

"A few days ago. I didn't pay much attention, to be honest."

Carol leant back in her chair and drew a deep breath. "You can't imagine how much better I feel," she said shakily. "I know it's silly, but I really got in a state about it. It seemed—threatening, somehow. But if you had one too, Stewart was probably right and it was just some yob going round the village with a felt pen."

"Well, if you're worried about anything in future, have a word with me before you start losing any sleep over it."

"Thanks, I might well do that."

Which, he felt, was as far as things should go for the moment. He glanced at his watch. "We'd better make a move or your family will be home before you, and since your car's in the drive, they'll wonder where you are."

"Yes." She bent to retrieve her purchases from the floor. "Thanks again for all your help—and for the tea. After a bad start, it's been a very pleasant afternoon."

Darren Barlow had arrived home, unannounced, for Easter, and his mother was trying to come to terms with the fact that she was less than pleased to see him.

"I should have thought you'd be busy at the pub over the holiday weekend," she said.

"Yeah, well, I decided I'd done my stint for this week and earned myself a rest." He was lounging on the sofa with his feet draped over the arm.

"You mean you've taken time off without permission?" Hazel's voice was concerned.

He grinned. "Got an upset stomach, haven't I?"

"Darren, if you start playing up they'll sack you, and then where—"

"Oh, shut it, Mum, for Pete's sake. I know what I'm

doing. Anyway," he added accusingly, "I thought you'd be glad to see me."

"I am, of course," Hazel said weakly, "but you might have let me know you were coming. We've been using your room for storage and it'll take a bit of sorting out. There's not much room, I'm afraid, what with Grandad and Mavis and Lenny."

He wasn't interested in her problems. "What's on up at the House? The car-park's thick with Rollers and Porsches."

"A wedding. I helped with the flowers. And there's a family party tomorrow, for Lord William's birthday. That's why the Opening's being held back till Monday."

Darren wasn't interested in Lord William either. He swung his feet to the ground and stood up. "I think I'll go to the pub and see who's around."

"There won't be anyone. It's not open."

He stopped, frowning. "Doesn't Stan know the law's changed? We're open all day at the Whistle Stop."

"It's different in Shillingham; there isn't the demand here. And before you go out, Darren, I'd be glad of a hand clearing your room. Some of those boxes are quite heavy."

"I came home for a rest, didn't I, not to start shifting furniture around."

"Up you go. It won't take long with two of us."

"I wish we still lived on the top road," he grumbled, allowing himself to be propelled up the narrow staircase. "There's not room to swing a cat here."

"You've never known any different," Hazel said shortly.

"Doesn't mean I have to like it, or that toffee-nosed lot who've moved in. And as for Dad going along and doing their bloody gardens for them—"

"Now that's enough. Help me lift these cases off the bed. We'll just have to stack them against the wall for now."

"I saw that poncy twit from the Schoolhouse as I arrived," he went on, manoeuvring his end of the case.

"Made him skip out of the way as I came round the corner." He grinned sourly. "Probably the only exercise he's had in weeks!"

While Giles Parrish wouldn't have recognized himself from Darren's description, he was equally scathing about the young lout in the crash helmet who'd taken the corner too fast.

"Damn nearly hit me," he complained to his wife. "Young fool! No doubt he was one of those making all that row the other night. I'm only sorry I didn't get his number."

"Well, I'm glad you didn't," Lalage retorted. "If you reported him, we might well have more than graffiti to worry about."

"Meaning he'd try to get his own back? I'm not going to be intimidated by young hooligans. If someone doesn't make a move to control them, they could get really out of hand."

"Look, Giles, I don't want us to get involved—right? We're working flat out to get the business off the ground, and the last thing we need is hassle at home. We bought this place as a retreat, remember, somewhere to unwind away from the big city. If you're going to start antagonizing the locals, we'd have been better staying in Bristol."

"Antagonizing! Ye gods, all I did was cross the road! I could have been *killed*, dammit!" He stared at her, aggrieved. "A little sympathy wouldn't have gone amiss."

She turned to look at him, trying to see him as the motorcyclist had: small, pointed beard, narrow eyes behind rimless tinted glasses, a thick brush of hair. Not, admittedly, a typical villager, in his designer jeans, silk shirt and cravat. No doubt it was amusing to make him leap clear.

"OK, love, I'm sorry. Go and sit on the patio and I'll bring out a G & T."

"That's more like it!"

Giles went through the double-glazed doors and seated

himself on the bench with a small sigh. He knew that the burglary up the road had disturbed Lalage, as had the drunken brawl the other night. Life in the country wasn't quite the panacea they'd been led to expect. All the same, it was very peaceful at the back here and he felt himself relax as he gazed out over the garden.

Their share of the converted school and its grounds was roughly two-thirds, and the expanse in front of him had once been the playing field. Now, beds of tulips and daffodils lay on either side of a smooth lawn, and young trees had been planted to provide shade.

Lalage came through the doors behind him, with a clinking of ice against glass. She put the tray down and joined him on the bench. "This is the life! Another month or so, and we'll be able to have supper out here."

"Yes, I was just thinking how peace—"

Behind the fence to their right a door opened suddenly, and raised voices drowned the end of his sentence. "Of course I didn't think of it—why should I?" The Parrishes looked at each other with raised eyebrows. Mrs.—Dexter, wasn't it? In the background her husband's voice, though equally angry in tone, was undecipherable. Then hers again, clear and shrill.

"Well, it was your fault for leaving it out . . . *What* 'should I have known'? That no one in this hateful place can be trusted? It's all right for you, swanning off every morning . . . Yes, it *is* relevant! I was glad to have someone to talk to, if you must know. Just as I was today, with Mr. Carey. And that's what this is really all about, isn't it? The fact that he took me to Lethbridge and we spent the afternoon together. Well, it was more than you were prepared to do, so you've only yourself to blame."

There was a sound of something being dropped into a dustbin and the crashing of its lid, followed by the slam of the back door. Then silence.

"Well, well!" Lalage said softly. "That was a bit of an eye-opener!"

"Particularly as it's the first squeak we've heard from them. She's always seemed such a quiet little thing."

"It sounds as if the solitude's getting to her. I don't blame her; I'd go nuts if I had to stay here all day."

"I wonder what Carey was doing taking her to town?" mused Giles.

His wife laughed. "Wouldn't you like to know! Come on, let's move inside. It's getting a bit chilly now and there's a programme I want to watch on TV."

She went back through the open doors, but her husband stood for a moment gazing reflectively at the fence before picking up the tray and following her.

# CHAPTER 4

Easter Monday, and, surprisingly for a bank holiday, it was still sunny. Which, Alison reflected, would probably mean quite a crowd at the House this afternoon. Usually she looked forward to holiday weekends, when the family could be together. However, Jonathan had gone to Paris for Easter with a group of friends, and, with her mind in a turmoil, Neil's presence round the house was a constant irritant. She glanced at him across the breakfast table, his nose buried in the paper. Beside him, Pippa tapped unenthusiastically at her egg.

"Anyone any plans for the day?" Alison asked with forced brightness.

Neil merely grunted but Philippa looked up, her large brown eyes mournful. "We *were* going to the point-to-point, but Rick's got to visit his grandparents. I was really looking forward to it, too."

"I'll go with you," Alison volunteered, feeling her spirits lift. The perfect solution.

"Will you really, Mum?" Pippa brightened visibly. "That'd be great!"

Neil lowered his paper. "Does that mean I'll be left alone yet again?"

"You can come too," Alison said blithely, knowing he wouldn't. Her love of horses, which Pippa had inherited, was definitely not shared by her husband.

"If I'm to be bored rigid, it might as well be in comfort."

"Never mind, Daddy—only one more day, and you'll be back at work!" Pippa winked mischievously at her mother. "We'll need a picnic lunch," she added. "What have we got?"

"Cold chicken and apple pie from yesterday. Don't worry"—as Neil moved protestingly—"there'll be plenty left for you. And if you're stuck for something to do, dear, there are several trays of bedding plants needing attention."

"But what about the Opening?" Neil objected. "Shouldn't you be here?"

"Public openings are not my concern," Alison reminded him. "Old Mr. Barlow will be on the gate as usual. I saw them putting up the kiosk before breakfast."

"Well, all I can say is it's been a damn-awful weekend!" he said forcefully, pushing his chair back and scraping the wall. Alison looked after him as he strode from the room, aware that any guilt she might have felt had been expunged by Daphne's revelations. Then, with a little sigh, she went to help Philippa pack their lunch.

At Coppins Farmhouse, too, there was an air of tension. Carol closed the lid of the children's suitcase, fighting back tears. She didn't want them to go camping; she wanted them here with her, company for the next two weeks. But it was all arranged now, and there was nothing she could do about it. Furthermore, after the row with Stewart last night she'd opted out of driving up to his sister's with them. Now, she regretted it. At least it would have got her out of the house for the day. But she had never got on with Rachel, and in his present mood, she didn't want Stewart's exclusive company on the way home either. Oh, damn *everything!* she thought miserably, and before she could stop herself, wondered what Mr. Carey was doing today.

"Mummy!" Jenny's impatient voice sounded from the hall. "Is the case ready? Daddy says it's time we were going."

Carol brushed her hand across her eyes. "Just coming." Normally Stewart carried the luggage downstairs, but today he was leaving it to her. Gritting her teeth, she staggered down with it and dropped it with a thud on the hall carpet. James slid his hand inside hers.

"I'd rather stay here with you, Mummy," he said in a small voice. She bent quickly and pulled him against her, squeezing her eyes shut against the renewed threat of tears.

"You'll have a lovely time, darling, and you can tell me all about it when you come home."

"Come on, then." Stewart lifted the case and went with it out of the front door, on which the faint outline of the face was still discernible. "I don't know what time I'll be back," he added over his shoulder. "Depends on the traffic, and whether or not I'm expected to stay for supper."

She wouldn't beg him to hurry home. She wouldn't. But if he'd turned at that moment and asked her to go with them, she wouldn't have hesitated. Instead she stood alone at the front door, waving to the two little figures at the rear window until the car turned out on to the road and disappeared from sight. It was ten-thirty, and from what Stewart had said, it could be twelve hours before he returned. She knew he was still angry with her and wouldn't hurry on her account.

"What'll I tell them?" he'd demanded, when she had stated her intention of remaining at home.

"Whatever you like. Say your boss is coming for dinner tomorrow and I've things to prepare. It's true, anyway."

And that, she thought determinedly, was what she

would do. She'd clean the house from top to bottom, she'd have another go at removing that odious outline from the front door, and then she'd start on the pastry-making and marinating. Somehow the hours would pass. She turned and went back into the house, carefully locking the front door behind her.

"There's a great deal of traffic all at once," Edith Irving remarked from the window. "That's the third coach that's gone past in as many minutes. Where are they all going?"

"Beckworth House, I should think," Gina replied. "It's open this afternoon. Shall we wander along?"

Bob said with a grin, "As long as it doesn't give you ideas above your station!"

"I'd like to see the gardens; I need a bit of inspiration for that back bed."

"It'll be very crowded," her mother observed, "judging by all those cars. I'm not sure I want to be jostled from pillar to post."

"Well, if you'd rather I could go with you another time. It's open on Wednesdays too, which are probably less crowded."

"And someone will have to stay in for the boys," Edith added reprovingly.

"No need for that," Bob countered. "They have their keys, and we can leave a note saying where we are. So, are we going or not?"

Gina hesitated, torn as always between her own wishes and consideration for her mother. "I would like to—"

"Then let's go. How about you, Ma?"

"No, I think I'll wait till Wednesday, thank you."

"Nice to have you to myself," Bob remarked, as they strolled down the road. "It's like a half-holiday from school!"

"I hope she doesn't mind being left alone."

"She had the choice, but she never agrees to anything

without an in-depth study of the pros and cons. The opposite of impulsive, your mother."

Another couple of coaches overtook them and turned into Tinker's Lane. Just inside the open gates of the House a wooden barrier had been erected, blocking access except for a narrow opening alongside a small kiosk. At its window, Gina recognized the old man in the wheelchair whom she'd seen around the village.

"House and gardens or gardens only?" he asked.

"The lot, please. Two."

"Like a brochure as well?"

"Yes, please," Gina said.

"Extortion!" Bob commented, handing her the brochure. "Why do you want that?"

"It'll give the family history and a plan of the House. We can use it every time we come. Look at these fantastic photographs. I'd no idea it was so lush inside."

They followed the stream of people up the winding drive, Gina reading snippets from the guide book as they went. "The Dukes of Hampshire have lived here for five hundred years," she stated, "though the original house was destroyed by fire in 1680. The present building is an early example of England's great Palladian country houses. The ceiling of the Great Hall—"

"Sorry to interrupt," Bob said, "but if we hurry we can tag on to the end of the tour that's just starting. Otherwise we have to wait for half an hour." And, taking her arm, he hurried her over to the small crowd grouped in front of the House.

The noise level which assaulted Joe Barlow as he entered his kitchen caused a spasm of actual pain in his ears. Darren and several of his cronies were lounging on all the available furniture, cans of beer in their hands, while they shouted at each other above the excruciating noise of the transistor. Joe strode into the room and switched off the set. The silence was almost as deafening, throbbing in his head in a blessed cessation of sound.

Darren straightened aggressively. "Why'd you do that, Dad? We were listening to it."

"So was half Beckworth, I should think. This is a private house, not a disco. Mrs. Evans next door must have been vibrating in time to that lot—it's a wonder we haven't had people knocking on the door. Not," he added drily, "that you'd have heard them if they had."

"OK, so we'll turn the volume down." Darren uncurled himself from the sofa and moved towards the set, but his father forestalled him.

"Hang on a minute. What are you all doing here anyway?"

"We came back when the pub shut. Nothing wrong with that, is there?"

Joe sighed. The boy's aggressive attitude was hard to stomach, but he'd no wish to give him a dressing-down in front of his pals. "At least you could go to your room—"

But even as he spoke, Joe saw the hole he had dug for himself.

"My room?" Darren jeered. "I can hardly fit into it myself, let alone with anyone else. And this *is* my home, isn't it? Where else should I take my friends?"

"Where are your mother and Mavis?" Joe asked, evading the question.

"Don't know. The place was empty when we got here."

Joe looked helplessly round the room. There was nowhere for him to sit, even if he'd wished to stay. And he'd been looking forward to a relaxing afternoon at home.

"It's not *my* fault if you want to live in a matchbox," Darren went on belligerently. "But if I'm not welcome I can always go back to the Whistle Stop."

"All right, boy, that's enough. As you say, it's your home. Just don't destroy it with that ghetto-blaster." And, turning on his heel, he left the house again, though not before he had caught the self-satisfied smirk on his son's face.

But the boy was right, he thought grimly, trudging back up the Lane. There *wasn't* enough room for them all at Number 17, even without Darren. And when the baby arrived, probably crying in the night and disturbing them all, it would be even worse. Yet he couldn't have turned Mavis out when she married, and of course her husband should be with her.

What was *wrong* with the world, he wondered helplessly, when folk couldn't afford homes in their own villages? The last few years had been disastrous for Beckworth, first the shop closing, then the school. They'd been the heart of village activity; now, all that was left was the pub. Ten years ago, there'd have been a good job here for Darren and he'd never have got in with that bad Shillingham crowd. Was he still on drugs? Joe wondered uneasily. Lord, what a mess everything was. If only they hadn't had to leave Coppins. But it was no use thinking of that now.

He crossed the road opposite the car-park—nearly full, he noted—and turned the corner by the gates of the House. People were still streaming into the drive. With a nod at his father, busily at work, Joe moved the barrier aside and slipped through, replacing it behind him. Might as well fill in his time with a bit of gardening. It usually soothed him when his nerves were frayed.

Branching off among the trees, he made his way to the tool-shed.

Carol, too, had been aware of the flow of traffic to Beckworth House. As she polished the sewing-table in the window she watched the coaches rolling past, lined with curious faces which peered over her fence. They'd be a mixed bunch, these sightseers, she thought uneasily. Perhaps from their elevated viewpoint they were considering which houses would be worth burgling. What was it Mr. Carey had said? *You get all kinds of weirdos.*

Determinedly she dismissed them from her mind and, the cleaning done, moved into the kitchen to prepare for the dinner party.

It was four-thirty when she next glanced at the clock, and by then the traffic had long since dwindled to a trickle. There'd still be about an hour, though, before the House closed. She stood for a moment, considering, then reached a decision. She was bored with her own company, and she'd done what she set out to do: the house was gleaming, and everything which could be prepared in advance for the next evening had been completed. She would go and have a look at the Stately Home.

Pulling off her apron, she draped it over the back of a chair, picked up her handbag and, since the day had clouded over, slipped on her raincoat. There was time for a quick look round, and perhaps, if Neil Carey saw her pass his windows, he might come out and join her.

A group of late sightseers was filing through the gates as she reached them, and she joined on the end of the line. Then, slipping her admission ticket into her pocket, she set off up the drive, against the general tide of people who were already making their way back to the gates.

Because of the time factor she'd paid only to visit the gardens, but at the top of the drive the House came into view and she paused to study it, admiring the gracious façade, the arched windows and mellow stone.

From the plethora of signposts pointing in all directions, it was clear that an entire day could be passed pleasantly here. Idly, Carol read a few of them: Gift Shop, Antique Market, Walled Garden, Lily Pond. Which one should she follow? As she hesitated, she caught sight of a familiar figure disappearing round a bend in one of the paths. Her decision made for her, she quickened her footsteps and hurried after him.

Although Summer Time had started, it had been dark for over an hour when Stewart Dexter turned off the M4 at the Shillingham exit, and he felt a twinge of guilt. There was no need to be this late and it was particularly unfair when Carol was so nervy. But he'd been embarrassed at having to explain her absence to his sister, whose knowing look confirmed that she suspected a family row. True, there had been one; but looking back, things hadn't been right between them since they came to Beckworth. Carol was continually on edge, though he was damned if he could see why. She'd never worried in London, even when he'd had to go abroad on business for weeks at a time. He couldn't imagine why she'd not settled in the village. Damn it, they'd done up the house exactly as she wanted, and it had cost enough.

Admittedly she hadn't any friends there, but she'd not tried to make any. On the contrary, she'd refused point-blank to go to tea at the vicarage, even though he'd assured her she wouldn't be immediately press-ganged into the Mothers' Union.

With a sigh, he turned off the Lethbridge road and started to climb the hill. It was very dark under the trees, and he turned up his headlamps. A pair of bright eyes shone in their glare, then disappeared. Unaccountably, he shivered. God, he was as bad as Carol! He put his foot down, taking the winding road dangerously fast.

Young James had been tearful when he left, and he remembered the child's sudden clinging to Carol that morning. It struck him for the first time that she might have welcomed the children's company during the holidays. It was decent of her to have raised no objection to the trip. Bless her, he thought uncomfortably, that might well have been the cause of her jumpiness this last week. He should have been more understanding.

The road opened out and he was glad to have left the trees behind. Lamps glowed welcomingly along the road and he was able to dip his headlights again. He'd open a bottle of wine, he thought suddenly, to make amends. An apology would probably be in order, too. Full of good intentions, he swung the car into his drive, then stared disbelievingly at the house. It was in complete darkness.

Immediately his irritation returned. She must have gone to bed early; but hell, she could have left the hall light on. The headlights lit his way into the garage, but he had to manoeuvre the front-door key into the lock, since any light from the street was obscured by the high fence. As he pushed open the door, the air felt warm and he detected a lingering smell of herbs and garlic. Preparations for tomorrow, no doubt. So that hadn't been only an excuse. He switched on the hall light.

"Carol?"

There was silence, and he knew with some sixth sense that the house was empty. Nevertheless he went into each room, one after the other, switching on all the lights. As he'd suspected, she was in none of them. The bedroom was exactly as he'd seen it that morning, the duvet plumped and neatly folded back to air the bed. She must have decided to teach him a lesson; probably gone into Shillingham or Lethbridge to the cinema. But, he remembered uneasily, her car was in the garage. Perhaps that bloody man from the Lodge had taken her out again.

Going back downstairs, he noticed that her handbag, which, when she was in the house, invariably stood on the hall table, was missing. A glance into the cloakroom confirmed that her raincoat had also gone. That was it, then. She was off somewhere enjoying herself. He was all the more aggrieved because he'd been prepared to apologize. All right, stuff her, if that was the way she wanted to play it.

He walked into the brightly lit sitting-room, crossed to the bar and poured himself a drink. In here the overriding smell was of polish, and the furniture gleamed richly. Obviously she'd been home most of the day.

The sound of an approaching car took him swiftly to

the window, but it didn't stop. Angrily he swished the curtains closed, turned on the television and sat down, glass in hand, to wait for her.

Alison undressed slowly, her mind on the events of the day just passed. The point-to-point had been enjoyable, and Philippa's pleasure unalloyed. She herself, though, had had to keep dragging her mind back to the present, to the beautiful lines of horse and rider, the countryside and the sunshine. Left to themselves, her thoughts slid inexorably to Neil and Daphne Warrender. What exactly had happened before his enforced "redundancy"? On past experience it was almost certain a woman was involved. But which? A wife of one of the directors? A secretary? Someone she'd met? Sick with humiliation and the anger she was unable to express, her resolution not to confront Neil with her knowledge had begun to weaken.

And was their marriage really worth saving? she wondered now. She'd never be able to trust him again. Perhaps, now the children were able to cope, it would be better to separate and salvage some chance of happiness. Though she hadn't realized it, the last three years had been borrowed time, and the mental strain of yet again trying to forgive and forget was too much to contemplate.

On the other hand, as she'd decided by the pond, she could wait till Neil again brought up the subject of moving.

Her tired brain teased at the problem, swinging first one way then the other. At last, still undecided, she climbed into bed and determinedly went to sleep.

## CHAPTER 5

By the next morning, Stewart's anger was mixed with unease. He'd slept only fitfully, constantly listening for Carol's return, and by six o'clock was showered, dressed and pacing the floor. Staying out all night was a different matter from a possible visit to the cinema. Surely she hadn't *left* him? A frantic look in the bathroom revealed that her toothbrush was still in the rack, but that meant nothing. She had a special travelling one which she always took on holiday. As for her make-up, how the hell could he tell if she'd taken any of that with her?

At nine o'clock he phoned his office and announced tersely that he would be late in. Then, schooling his voice to casual inquiry, he rang first Carol's mother, then Sue Kingdom. Neither of them had seen or heard from her in the last twenty-four hours, and the immediate alarm in their voices did nothing to calm him. "We had a slight tiff," he explained unwillingly. "I took the children to Rachel's and she refused to come with us, and when I got home she wasn't here."

Having promised them both to ring as soon as Carol came back, Stewart replaced the phone and stood thinking. A suitcase. Could she have taken one? But if she'd intended staying away, surely she'd have taken her car? Only then, with a cold feeling in his stomach, did he remember he'd not yet recharged its battery. The car's presence didn't mean a thing; she couldn't have used it anyway.

Going up the stairs two at a time, he opened the box-room door and stood surveying the collection of trunks, cases and grips from which, only the previous morning, Carol herself had extracted the children's suitcase. Had that given her the idea? And had she taken another out, later, for her own use? To his frustration he could not tell if one was missing.

Downstairs again and out into the road. Standing at the gate, he looked to right and left, half expecting to see her come walking towards him. He was tempted to knock on a few doors, ask if she'd been seen, if a taxi had called, but he refrained. He hardly knew anyone here, and didn't want to look a fool. And what in heaven's name could he say, anyway?

Eventually he went back into the house, wrote a note saying, "Please phone the office as soon as you get back. Love, Stewart" and propped it prominently on the hall table. Then, with a last helpless look round, he went out to the car and belatedly set off for London.

That evening, Shillingham police received two phone-calls from Beckworth. The first, from a Mr. Giles Parrish, reported a break-in while he and his wife had been at work; the second, from Stewart Dexter, that his wife was missing.

What the hell had got into that village all of a sudden? Alan Crombie thought irritably. In response to the first call he arranged for Sage, accompanied by Sally Pierce since Perry was down with 'flu, to go and interview the householders. The list of burglaries was growing daily, he reflected gloomily, and there was still no lead. The second call he ignored, knowing it had been dealt with by the desk sergeant and passed to him only for information.

"I'm sorry, sir," Sergeant Fenton had told Stewart, "it's much too soon to initiate inquiries. From what you say, your wife might well have taken a suitcase with her, which would make it a voluntary disappearance. In any event she took her coat and handbag, which shows she wasn't just popping out to the post. Yes, sir, I appreciate that you're worried, but I'm afraid this happens all the time."

He listened while Stewart explained about the dinner-party. "We'd some important guests coming this evening, and my wife had prepared two of the courses. She wouldn't have gone to that trouble if she'd been intending to go away."

To Fenton, whose wife never prepared a meal until they were about to eat it, this proved exactly the opposite, but he didn't say so. "Look, sir, we're always getting calls saying someone's wife or husband has disappeared, but they almost always turn up again in a day or two. I'm sure it will be the same for you."

In the police car Sally Pierce sat primly, knees together, as far from her companion as possible. She didn't like Harry Sage, who had leered at her more than once and made suggestive remarks, but he was her superior and she wasn't in a position to tell him to go to hell. At the moment, fortunately, his mind was on the job.

"I'm wearing a track to this bloody village," he said moodily, "and a chi-chi place it is nowadays. Been there lately, Sal?"

Sally, who intensely disliked being called Sal, shook her head.

"It's been prettied up and gentrified, and if you ask me, its life-blood has been sucked out of it. They all live behind high hedges and fences and don't even know the names of their next-door neighbours. Not much community spirit, I can tell you."

Sally made a non-committal reply and looked out of the window at the primrose-starred verges. She loved this time of year, when the trees were bedecked with blossom and the tender green of new growth showed in the hedgerows. As they drove up through the tunnel of trees, she hoped fervently that they'd be back down the hill before dark. She wouldn't put it past Sage to turn the car into one of these sheltered pathways.

"Anyway," he was continuing, "I don't know why we're wasting our time on this. Should be turned over to Regional Crime, lock, stock and barrel."

The latest burglary victim was awaiting them at his

gate, a striking figure with goatee beard and rimless tinted glasses. The bloke they'd missed last time, presumably.

"Bloody infuriating!" he greeted them as they got out of the car. "They've taken my brand-new music centre and a caseful of compact discs. Must have had a ruddy great van standing by to load it into. It's a wonder the old folks next door didn't notice it."

"I'm surprised you haven't an alarm system, sir," Sage said in gentle rebuke. "I'm Detective-Sergeant Sage and this is Miss Pierce."

Parrish nodded absently. "We'd never thought it necessary, out here in the sticks. We'll get one now, though, after the horse has gone. Becoming a high-risk area, isn't it, two in less than a week."

"It's possible a motorway gang's involved. The North Park and Hatherley districts of Shillingham have also been hit."

"Well, let's hope you nab them. I suppose you want a statement of some kind? Your fingerprint chaps are all over the house, but my wife's in the back garden. Shall we go and join her?"

They walked round the side of the house adjacent to Coppins Farmhouse to an immaculate and colourful garden. Lalage Parrish was on the terrace, watching the Scenes of Crime men through the patio doors. She turned at their approach, a pale, gaunt woman with huge eyes and hollow cheeks, whose unlikely shade of hair—a deep copper—emphasized rather than lessened the wanness of her appearance. She was dressed in a fashionable version of a painter's smock, and her designer jeans were a his 'n' hers replica of her husband's.

Parrish performed the introductions, and they seated themselves on the garden bench while Sally made notes. His wife's main concern was some missing jewellery; a heavy gold pendant studded with turquoise, a cameo brooch and a pair of diamond earrings.

Harry Sage sat listening to the woman's low voice and

the scratching of Sally's pen. The early evening sunshine lay slantingly over the grass and lit the tulips to a glowing red. There was a froth of blossom on the cherry trees, and somewhere overhead a lark filled the sky with liquid music. He sighed, recalling his attention as the woman stopped speaking.

"And as far as you know, that's all they've taken?" he summarized.

"All?" Lalage Parrish raised her eyebrows. "It's enough, surely? I hope you can get it back for us."

Sage was glad she didn't know the odds on that one.

"I trust they know what they're doing," Lalage remarked, when Giles returned from seeing the police out. "I didn't much care for the man. Too cocky by half."

"Oh, they think they know it all, these fellows, but the crime figures prove them wrong."

She turned to peer through the window again. "I wish they'd hurry up in there. I'm in need of a gin."

Out in the road, Sage was about to get in the car when Stewart Dexter came hurrying from the next-door house.

"So they *did* take it seriously!" he exclaimed. "Thank God!"

Sage looked at him in surprise. "Good evening, Mr. Dexter. We always take burglaries seriously. I suppose you didn't hear anything of this one either? Your other neighbours this time!"

It was Dexter's turn to look blank. "You mean you haven't come about my wife?"

"Your wife, sir?"

"I phoned a couple of hours ago to report her missing."

"I'm sorry, sir," Sage said after a moment, "I know nothing about that."

The man's shoulders sagged. "She wouldn't just disappear without telling me, particularly with the dinner-party due."

Sally said rallyingly, "I'm sure there's some simple explanation, sir."

Dexter ran a hand through his fair curly hair. "I hope to God you're right," he said, and stood despairingly on the pavement as the police car drove away.

At nine o'clock the next morning Gina Cummings stood outside the locked gates of Beckworth House, wondering if she should ring the bell. As she hesitated, two women came down the short path from the Lodge, and thankfully she called to them.

Alison, walking towards her, wasn't sure for a moment who she was. Then she remembered: the woman from Mews Grange.

"I'm sorry to trouble you," Gina began, "but I've only just heard about Mrs. Dexter."

"Who?"

"Our next-door neighbour. She's gone missing. Her husband told mine just now, as he was leaving for work. He's been on to the police, but it seems they're not taking it seriously. They think she might have gone of her own accord."

"Oh?" Alison waited in some bewilderment.

"But you see, I saw her on Monday afternoon. Here."

"Here?"

"In the grounds. We came to have a look round, and I caught sight of her walking up the drive."

"Did your husband tell Mr. Dexter?"

"No, he didn't know I'd seen her. She was some distance away, and it didn't seem worth mentioning at the time."

"Was she by herself?"

Gina nodded.

"And you're sure it was her?"

"Well—almost sure."

"So you think Mrs. Dexter was here on Monday afternoon, and she hasn't been seen since?"

"Yes, exactly. I was wondering if she could have had an

accident in the grounds somewhere? Fainted, or twisted her
ankle or something?"

"But it's almost two days ago! Surely she'd have attracted attention before this?"

"If she was conscious," said Gina, and shivered. "Are
the grounds patrolled?"

"Well, no, but we have a team of gardeners who cover a
pretty wide area."

"All the same, there must be parts of the grounds that
aren't visited every day."

"True. Right, if you think there's a chance she might be
out there we'd better start looking." She unlocked the small
inset gate and Gina walked through. "This is Mrs. Barlow;
I'm sure she'll help us."

Having unavoidably overheard the conversation, Hazel
nodded to Gina, her round eyes full of concern. She didn't
herself know the incomers along the top road, though of
course Joe did, being their milkman. "Poor lady," she murmured, "I do hope she's all right."

Alison held down a quiver of apprehension. *Could* someone have been lying out there all this time? It was an unnerving thought. Falling into step, the three women set out
on their macabre search.

There'd been a frost overnight, and under the trees it
still silvered the grass. "Let's go to the place where you saw
her," Alison suggested. "Then we can separate and look in
different directions. What time was it, would you say?"

"Quite late, just before we went home. About five, I
suppose. We'd had a cup of tea in the Orangery, and I know
that was at four-thirty, because Bob remarked that Mother
would be waiting for hers. Then when we came out we
went to the shop and I spent some time choosing pots of
herbs."

"So where was she when you saw her?"

"Just about where we are now. She'd come up the drive
and was standing looking at the House."

"If it was five o'clock she'd have been too late for a tour. So the question is, where did she go from here?"

"If it was me coming for the first time," Hazel said timidly, "I'd read all those signposts and follow one of them."

"Then let's do that." Alison ran her eye rapidly over them. "The gift shop's out. She couldn't have disappeared there, and the same goes for the antique market. The staff would have been there till they locked up. Which leaves the rose-garden, the walled garden and the lily-pond as the most likely places. If those are no good, we'll move on to the park, but we'll need an organized search-party for that. So—" She turned to Gina. "This is ridiculous—I don't know your name!"

"I'm so sorry—Gina Cummings."

"Then would you take the rose-garden, Hazel the walled garden, and I'll start with the lily-pond. And if you see any gardeners on your travels, press-gang them to join us. If we've no luck, we'll meet back here and decide what to do next."

"And what if we do find her?" Gina asked nervously.

"Yell for the rest of us. We'll all keep an ear open." She paused. "In all probability she's back home by now, drinking a cup of coffee. And I have to say I wish I was."

They nodded sombrely at each other, then turned and set off in their appointed directions. She'd come this way on Saturday, Alison reflected, after hearing Daphne's bombshell. Now, she walked slowly, heart beating with apprehension, between the tall enclosing hedges and the wide flowerbeds that, in a month or two, would be a riot of colour. It was very still, and she wished suddenly that she hadn't suggested they separate, that all three of them were searching together. Yet if Mrs. Dexter had really been here since Monday, every minute could be crucial. Where had her husband been, Alison wondered inconsequentially, on a bank-holiday afternoon? It was usually a family time. Though in fact she hadn't been with her own husband, either.

She turned into the long straight avenue which led to the pond. High overhead an aeroplane droned lazily over the blue arc of the sky. There was no other, nearer sound. Irrationally, Alison wished she were in it, as moments before she'd wished she were drinking coffee at home. Anywhere, in fact, but here, engaged in this disturbing search.

As she walked, looking from side to side, she called softly, unwilling to raise her voice in the oddly churchlike silence. Occasionally she bent to peer under overhanging shrubbery, though surely if Mrs. Dexter had collapsed, it would have been on the path or close to it.

Emerging from the hemmed-in avenue to the open area of the pond, she drew a breath of relief. Seating herself on the bench as she had on Saturday, she ran her eyes slowly round the circumference of the water. There was nothing untoward. On the left-hand bank a group of mallards preened their feathers and across the water a family of moorhens swam self-importantly in single file.

For a moment or two Alison listened intently, in case one of the others should call. Silence. She was about to get up and go to meet them when a bird, swooping to land on a nearby lily-pad, took off again with a frightened squawk.

Curious to see what had startled it, Alison rose and walked to the edge of the pond, staring down into the dark water. For a blank, uncomprehending moment she thought it was her own reflection that shone back at her. But it was another face that floated there, glowing obscenely between the lily leaves, a white face with puckered skin and closed eyes and a weed trailing across one cheek.

Alison felt herself sway and stepped hastily back lest she too plunge to a watery grave. She stumbled back to the seat and sank gratefully on to it, gripping the wooden slats for support and fighting down a wave of nausea. She should call the others, she thought distractedly, but there was no hurry. Mrs. Dexter was past saving.

She had still not summoned the strength to stand when,

some minutes later, Hazel's voice reached her, close at hand.

"Mrs. Carey? There's no sign of her. Shall we—?"

Having rounded the corner with Gina Cummings, Hazel broke off abruptly.

Alison raised an ashen face. "In the pond," she said unsteadily. "Don't look—there's nothing we can do."

But Hazel, with a cry of concern, had started forward and was gazing with horror at the body floating below the lily-pads.

"But that's the young lady I saw on Saturday!" she exclaimed. "With Mr. Carey!"

Alison stared at her. "With *Neil?*"

"That's right. I was in the garden when they drove past. I thought how pretty she looked. And now—" Hazel choked to a halt.

Gina, who, though as white as the others, had wisely refrained from looking in the pond, took Alison's arm. "We'd better get to a phone," she said.

It was an hour later and the machinery for dealing with a major incident was rolling smoothly into place. The afternoon opening of House and gardens had been cancelled and a large notice to that effect was pinned on the gates. The drive was filled with an assortment of official cars, together with a hearse which, when the pathologist and Scenes of Crime officers had finished, would bear the body away. Meanwhile, an incident room was being set up in the village hall.

"No doubt it'll turn out to be a simple drowning," Sage told Sally, "but until the PM we won't know for sure, so we treat it as a suspicious death until we know different."

Sally nodded, resenting standard procedure being portrayed as his own decision. She said, "It's dreadful that there's no way of contacting the husband."

Sage snorted. "I told you about the 'I'm all right, Jack' mentality here. In the old days, everybody in the village would have known exactly where everyone else worked. Now, all anyone can come up with is 'London'. So the poor bugger has to come home to all this, with no cushioning of the blow. At least the kids are out of the way; Dexter told Cummings it was while he was taking them to his sister's that she disappeared."

Sally said soberly, "He thought we'd come to look for her last night."

"Well, we hadn't. It would have been too late by then, anyway. She must have been in the water since Monday. It's the only thing that makes sense."

The three women, having been separately interviewed by Sally and Sage, had come together again at the Lodge, somehow needing each other's company.

"I wonder how it happened?" Hazel said for the third time. "It's odd no one heard her fall: she must have called for help, surely?"

"It was nearly closing time," Alison reminded her. "Most people would already have left, and the pond is quite isolated. As to what happened, we'll never know, will we? She might have bent forward to look at something and toppled over. Or she could have felt faint and simply fallen in."

"Or," suggested Gina, hands round the warming mug of coffee, "a sudden noise might have startled her, making her jump and lose her balance. Is the water deep at the edge?"

"It shelves pretty steeply and the roots of the plants are thick below the surface. She could have become entangled with them. That's why there are notices all round the pond warning parents to keep hold of their children."

"Poor soul," Gina said, shuddering. "I was going to invite her for coffee this week; we've never been here long enough before."

Stewart Dexter, however, appeared to have no doubts about his wife's death. Arriving home to find the police car at his gate, he startled Sage with his wild cry: "She's killed herself, hasn't she? Where is she?"

Sage took his arm and, solemn-faced, accompanied him into the house, jerking his head towards the kitchen, which Sally took as an order to make tea.

In the sitting-room Stewart stood rigid, shaking off the detective's attempt to help him to a chair. "What *happened*, for God's sake?"

"She was found in the pond up at the House. I'm extremely sorry, sir."

Stewart looked at him blankly. "House? What house?"

"The Stately Home up the road."

"What was she doing there?"

"It was open to the public on Monday afternoon."

"What a strange place to choose," Stewart said, half under his breath.

Sage cleared his throat. "Why should you think she took her own life, sir?"

"Because she was frightened and unhappy and I didn't understand." The man's face was like marble and there was desperation in his eyes. "I should have had more sense than to leave her alone all day."

Sage, knowing from his previous visit that she'd been alone all day for the best part of six months, forbore to comment.

"The children going away must have been the last straw. I realized that on the way home; I intended to make it up to her. Now, I'll never have the chance." His voice broke and he turned away.

Where the hell was Sally with that tea? Though what the poor devil really needed was a stiff drink. "You say your wife was frightened, Mr. Dexter. Why was that?"

"She hated this place." Dexter stood at the window, hands rammed into his pockets, staring unseeingly across the sunlit patio. "She hated the loneliness, the unfriendliness. And she felt threatened by the village louts who whispered as she passed and drew graffiti on our door and fought on the pavement outside. And when she appealed to me, all I did was tell her to pull herself together and go off with the children, when I knew perfectly well that if I asked her again, she'd have come with us. And if she had, she'd still be alive."

There was no disputing that, at least. Sally arrived with a tea-tray and, at Sage's impatient nod, quickly poured out three cups. Dexter took one automatically, though he made no attempt to drink.

Sage said, "I'm afraid we'll have to ask you to come to Shillingham to identify her."

The man quivered, and some tea sloshed into his saucer. Sally said gently, "She looks very peaceful, sir."

Stewart turned and put the untouched cup of tea on the table beside him. "Then let's go," he said brusquely, "and get it over."

Alison said, "I'm afraid I've some bad news for you."

Neil, dropping his briefcase en route to the drinks cabinet, halted at the tone in her voice. "What is it?"

"A friend of yours was found dead today. In fact, I found her."

Neil stared at her, a sudden pulse jumping at his temple. "Is this some kind of joke?"

"I certainly didn't think so. She was drowned in the lily-pond."

"For God's sake, Alison! *Who* was drowned in the lily-pond?"

"Mrs. Dexter. Carol, wasn't it? Whom you took for a joy-ride on Saturday."

Neil moistened his lips. "You're saying Carol Dexter is dead?"

"I am."

"But God, that's terrible. What happened"?

"I told you. She drowned." She surveyed him critically. His face was livid and there was a shuttered look behind his eyes.

"But—when? And how did you come to find her?"

"Gina Cummings from Mews Grange called. She said Mrs. Dexter'd been missing since Monday, but she'd seen her here that afternoon. So we set out to look for her."

"And found her," Neil said softly.

"And found her." Alison paused, then added accusingly, "I didn't know you knew her."

"I hardly did."

"But you were together on Saturday afternoon. Hazel saw you."

"The good old grapevine." He was recovering his composure. "Her car battery was flat, and since she needed to get to Lethbridge, I gave her a lift."

"And stayed with her and brought her home again, no doubt."

"Well, a one-way trip wouldn't have been of much help, would it?"

"She was very pretty." Alison was banking on Hazel's comment, being unable to judge from the quick, horrified glance she'd had of Carol's dead face. But then, she thought caustically, Neil wouldn't have offered a lift to a plain woman.

"For pity's sake, Alison, I only did her a good turn! You're making it sound like a criminal offence."

"I'm just surprised you never mentioned it, if it was all so innocent."

"Because I wanted to avoid a scene like we're having now." He turned abruptly to the cabinet, sloshed whisky into two glasses and handed one to her.

"You must need this more than I do. What a dreadful experience. I suppose the police have been here?"

"Most of the day."

"I passed a Panda on the bottom road, and wondered briefly if there'd been another burglary. Poor girl," he added reflectively, staring into his glass. "She hated this place. Said nobody spoke to her from one week to the next."

"Gina Cummings was going to invite her for coffee."

"Too little, too late," said Neil bitterly, and Alison, the anger going out of her and a weary sadness taking its place, let the matter drop.

His comment, disconcertingly apt, was still in her mind when, a few hours later, she went up to bed, and she wished uselessly that poor Carol had at least known of the intended invitation before she met her death. Instead, she'd died in the cold water as lonely and unhappy as she'd apparently been living among them.

Switching off the light, she went to open the window. Immediately below was the outer wall of the estate and, across the road, the still-lit windows of the Green Man.

A car came swiftly up Tinker's Lane, its headlamps briefly lighting the dark corner of the car-park below her to reveal the shape of a car parked close against the wall. Then the moving car was past, and the other slipped back into obscurity.

Alison frowned. Odd: the car-park belonged to Beckworth House. The clientele of the Green Man, being mainly local, seldom arrived by car, but when they did, they parked in the pub forecourt. Curiously she pushed the sash wider and leaned out, craning her neck to see the shadowed vehicle more clearly. But from that angle all that was visible was the dark surface of its roof and bonnet.

A cool breeze rippled over her, and, abandoning her interest, she withdrew and let the curtain fall back into place.

# CHAPTER 6

The following morning, the post-mortem report disproved both Alison's and Stewart's hypotheses and the police had a case of murder on their hands.

"Bruise on the side of her face and a whacking great crack on the back of the head," Webb said, freely paraphrasing the medical report. "Stapleton says neither could have been caused by knocking against the edge of the pond. She was almost certainly unconscious when she hit the water."

"But not dead?" Crombie queried.

"No, diatoms in the bloodstream prove that."

"So she was knocked out by a blow to the head, whereupon her attacker picked her up and threw her in the pond."

"It seems so."

"Nice guy."

"He might have thought she was dead already."

"That makes a difference?"

Webb shrugged. "Not so that you'd notice." He stood up. "Well, Alan, the burglaries are all yours but this gem's been passed to me. Wish me luck with it."

Stewart Dexter, it appeared, had taken a few days' compassionate leave and driven up to break the news to his family. At Sage's request, he had left the name and address of a farm in the Cotswolds where the camping party was staying, and Webb arrived there with Sergeant Jackson in the middle of the afternoon.

The site was idyllic; a gently sloping meadow with a stream and a small wood at the foot and the cluster of white-washed farm buildings at the top. Four caravans in all were dotted round the field, each with its tents grouped about it. The farmer's wife advised them that the Davis family had the lower site on the left.

Leaving their car in the farmyard, the two detectives set off down the field, the wind in their hair and the burden of their news at variance with the relaxed holiday atmosphere.

That Dexter's own news had already taken its toll was evidenced by the strained face and red eyes of the woman who answered their knock on the caravan door.

"Mrs. Davis? Is Mr. Dexter there, please?"

A voice from behind her answered, "Yes, what is it?" and a tall, youngish man with fair curly hair and a white face appeared over her shoulder.

"Chief Inspector Webb and Sergeant Jackson, sir, Shillingham CID."

"My God, you don't give me much peace, do you? What is it now?"

"I'm afraid we have some news for you, sir." Webb hesitated. "Are your children in there?"

The woman answered. "No, my husband's taken all four of them out for the afternoon, to take their minds off things. You'd better come in."

The caravan was large and airy, with gaily patterned curtains at the open windows. On a table were a couple of mugs half full of tea. Mrs. Davis moved to the sink and refilled the kettle.

"Well, what is it?" Stewart Dexter demanded. "You can come straight out with it; nothing you say will make much difference now."

"I'm sorry to tell you, Mr. Dexter, that your wife's death wasn't an accident."

Pain crossed his face. "I'd guessed as much. She killed herself, didn't she?"

"No," Webb said steadily, "somebody else killed her."

Behind him the kettle clattered on the stove and he heard Mrs. Davis gasp.

Dexter hadn't moved. "Say that again?"

"Your wife was murdered, Mr. Dexter. I'm sorry."

Dexter felt behind him for a chair and lowered himself slowly into it. "How do you know?"

"Because she had injuries consistent with being attacked before going in the water."

"What kind of injuries?" His tone of voice betrayed what he feared. Webb could at least reassure him on that.

"Nothing sexual. A blow to the face and severe bruising and lacerations to the back of her head."

"You mean," he said incredulously, "someone simply walked up to her and *killed* her? But in God's name, why?"

"That's what we're trying to find out. It was probably a mugging; her bag was recovered from the pond this morning and the purse had been emptied. Any idea how much would have been in it?"

He shook his head dazedly. Mrs. Davis set cups and saucers in front of them and poured tea. Her hand, Webb noticed, was shaking.

"Her wrist-watch was missing too." Webb paused. "What time did you get home on Monday evening, sir?"

Dexter hesitated. "Around nine, I suppose."

Webb noted the sister's jerk of surprise, but she made no comment. "Which, since it's roughly an hour and a half's journey, means you left here at seven-thirty?" He was well in the clear, then; the estate gates were closed and locked soon after half past five.

"I drove back from Woodstock, not here," Dexter said. "They didn't come up till the next morning."

Webb had the impression it was an unwilling admission, made only because of his sister's presence. "Which would knock it down to—what?—an hour?"

"It depends on the traffic," the man said evasively.

"You left about eight, then?" Webb persisted, surprised by his reticence.

Dexter looked up, squaring his shoulders. "Actually it was before that. I'd intended to stay longer but my son was tearful, and I thought the sooner I left the better. I— stopped for a meal on the way home."

Webb raised an eyebrow. "Your wife wasn't expecting you for dinner?"

"I'd said I might be late. We usually stay for a meal with Rachel and Tom."

"So what time did you leave Woodstock, Mr. Dexter?"

"I really don't know. Fiveish, I suppose."

Webb stared at him, rapidly reassessing the situation. "Fiveish" was a fairly broad spectrum. If, for instance, he'd

left at a quarter to and had a clear run, it was just possible
he could have been back in Beckworth before the gates
closed.

Webb glanced at the woman. "Mrs. Davis? Can you tie
it down more closely?"

Flushing, she shook her head.

"So an hour's journey took you four hours, sir?"

"I told you I stopped for a meal. I didn't hurry over it."

"Obviously not." The man could stand more detailed
questioning, Webb thought, but not here. And if he *had*
reached Beckworth in time, would he have known where
his wife had gone?

"Did your wife mention visiting Beckworth House?"

"No; she said she was going to prepare for a dinner-
party we'd planned for the next evening."

"Had she ever shown any interest in it?"

"Not really. But she met the chap who lives at the
Lodge on Saturday. He gave her a lift into Lethbridge when
her car wouldn't start."

Webb digested that in silence. Then he asked mildly,
"Where were you at the time?"

"Out with the children."

They didn't seem a very close family, Webb thought.
Perhaps Dexter's obvious distress was due to a guilty con-
science. But how guilty?

"Forgive me, sir, but I have to ask: was it a happy marriage?"

Dexter looked up angrily. "What the hell has that to do
with anything?"

"Well, you certainly weren't in a hurry to get home on
Monday. I wondered if perhaps you'd had a disagree-
ment?"

Silence. Webb said quietly, "Or maybe you were in the
habit of quarrelling?"

The man's eyes filled with tears and he brushed them
angrily away. "Only since we moved to bloody Broadshire."

"Why was that?"

"Because Carol didn't settle as I'd hoped and expected. We paid a large sum for the house, and had it converted exactly to our taste. *Her* taste," he corrected himself. "But she didn't make any friends and she complained of being lonely."

According to Sage's report, the woman had also been afraid. "You told my colleague she was frightened. What of, exactly?"

"The village boys, mainly. They're a scruffy bunch, given to lounging around on corners and making comments as you pass. It can be quite unnerving." His mouth twisted. "We called them the Beckworth Bruisers."

"Did they actually threaten her in any way?"

"Oh, I don't think so. She was just being neurotic." He broke off. "At least, that's what I thought. My God, you mean one of them might have killed her?"

"At this stage, sir, anyone might." He paused. "This gentleman who gave her a lift; do you know his name?"

"Carey. His wife's the booking manager, Carol said."

"You haven't met him yourself?"

"No."

"And as far as you're aware, he's the only person in the village with whom she had any contact?"

"Apart from the vicar and the tradesmen, yes."

"How long are you staying here, Mr. Dexter?"

"A couple of days, but I won't be returning to Beckworth. I'm going back to London and the children will stay with Rachel while I decide what to do." He paused and added sullenly, "If you have no objection?"

"Not as long as we know where to contact you," Webb said smoothly.

"I'll be staying with a Mr. and Mrs. Kingdom." Their address and phone number were duly noted by Jackson.

"And if you could give us the name of the place where you ate on Monday?"

Dexter flushed a dull red. "The Buttery, in Swindon."

"Thank you. Now, will you be leaving a key with anyone? We shall want to examine your wife's belongings; there might possibly be a lead there."

Dexter seemed about to protest, then shrugged and, taking his key-ring from his pocket, detached a key and handed it over. "I've a spare one at the office."

"Thank you very much, sir." Webb finished his tea and signalled to Jackson, who closed his notebook. "And thanks for the tea, Mrs. Davis. I'm sorry to have been the bearer of more bad news."

"A pretty rum story, Guv," Jackson commented when they were back in the car. "What do you reckon he was up to?"

"I don't know, Ken, but I intend to find out. First thing tomorrow, ring that Buttery place. They'd have been busy on Easter Monday and I'll be surprised if they let anyone spin a meal out for three hours. In the meantime, since we've got the key on us we'll go and take a look at the house."

It was barely five days since Webb had driven up the hill, but this time he was in no mood to admire the scenery. Ironic that after visiting the village for the first time in years, it should immediately feature in a murder case.

"I detailed Sage and Pierce to do the preliminaries," he said. "They've already met several of the people up there, which could be useful."

"Same lot as were involved in the burglaries?" Jackson inquired.

"Not the dead woman, but neighbours on both sides."

"You reckon there's a connection?"

"You tell me, Ken." They had emerged from the wood now and were entering the village. It didn't seem as peaceful as it had on Saturday, possibly due to the presence of blue-uniformed figures on doorsteps. House-to-house inquiries were under way.

"Where are we looking for, Guv?"

"Coppins Farmhouse. It should be along here on the right. Yes, here we are."

The five-barred gate, relic of a previous existence, was firmly closed. Jackson unlatched it and the two men walked through into the gravelled driveway. The old house, its gable-end facing them, waited impassively. To their right a patio lay spread in the sun, its tubs of flowers and shrubs bright splashes of colour. Apart from the gap of the gateway, the village was completely obscured by the high fence that fronted the property. If these new villagers prized their privacy so highly, they shouldn't be surprised if no one spoke to them.

He took Dexter's key from his pocket and fitted it into the lock. The door, highly polished for the most part, had an area of dull wood in the centre. Peering more closely, Webb could just make out a faint circle, which someone had apparently attempted to remove. Kids! he thought resignedly, pushing the door open.

Already the house smelt stuffy and unused, but the carpets were spotless and the wood of an old chest glowed luminously from the shadows. As Webb moved from one room to another, Jackson risked a quick glance at his watch. After five already. He'd hoped to be home early this evening; they'd had a disturbed night, with young Paul vomiting and complaining of stomach ache, and as he left home that morning, Millie had been phoning the doctor.

"Ken?"

He hurried into the long, low-ceilinged sitting-room. "Yes, Guv?"

"Have a quick look through this desk, will you. Cheque stubs, bank statements, address books—the usual thing. I'll go through the dressing-table drawers. More complicated with a woman; you never know where they'll hide things."

The staircase was wide and shallow, carpeted in old-rose Wilton. Webb paused at the top, surveying the corridor which stretched in front of him with innocently open doors. When Mrs. Dexter had left the house, he reflected, she hadn't realized it would be for the last time. It was possible, therefore, that she might have left something lying around which would otherwise have been hidden.

Webb walked into the main bedroom with its bathroom *en suite*. Here the furniture was modern and, in his opinion, inappropriate to the age of the house. Cream and gold wardrobes lined the walls, and a long bemirrored dressing-table stood under one window. He walked across, sat down on the stool and opened one drawer after another. They revealed nothing out of the ordinary; a sachet of lace handkerchiefs, several pairs of tights, some underwear in soft pastel shades. The centre drawer was much as he remembered his wife's: a jumble of lipsticks, some without tops, eye-shadows and blushers, and an open box of face-powder whose contents coated everything with a layer of pink dust.

Webb sighed, pushing the drawer shut. It was at times like this that "the deceased" became a real woman, one who had stood before this mirror appraising her appearance, had slept in that bed and stood, perhaps, at this window, gazing out on an alien landscape. Carol Dexter had been afraid, and with reason; though whether her fear had been directed against the right person remained to be seen. But as far as he could tell there were no secret letters hidden away up here. Not even a diary in the bedside table, though such an accessible place would not in any case have held anything private.

He stood in the centre of the room taking a last look round, at the ruched blinds at the window—another anachronism—and the lemon silk negligée on the back of the door. A feminine room, and one which he could understand Stewart Dexter fleeing from once its other occupant had gone.

Returning downstairs, Webb went into the kitchen and, noticing the humming of the fridge, opened its door. A covered casserole stood on one shelf, a rich, creamy mousse on another. The ill-fated dinner-party. These preparations must have been the last tasks Carol Dexter performed.

"Ken!"

"Yes, Guv?" Jackson materialized beside him. "Nothing much in the desk, and what there is seems to be Mr. Dexter's."

Webb nodded absently. "We'll leave it to the SOCOs then. I'm wondering about this fridge. It shouldn't be left on if no one's here."

Jackson in his turn looked inside. "Shall I put whatever will fit into the freezer? That's what Millie does when we go on holiday."

The sound of the doorbell reached them and, leaving Jackson to attend to the fridge, Webb went to answer it. Harry Sage stood outside.

"I saw the car," he said, "and wondered if you needed any help."

"I don't think so, thanks. We've just about finished here, then we'll wander up the road and have a look round. Any more developments?"

"They've found where the attack took place. Traces of blood on one of those low, metal urns beside the path."

"Is it near the pond?"

"Yes, only a few yards away."

"So he had a convenient dumping place close by." He paused. "You met the murdered woman, didn't you? What was she like?"

"Bit of all right, actually. Nice figure, pretty, well dressed."

"I meant her manner," Webb said caustically.

Sage flushed. "Oh. Well, she was pretty jittery. Bundle of nerves, in fact. Her husband was a bit short with her."

"There was an atmosphere between them?"

Sage frowned, thinking back. "Well, nothing exceptional. He corrected her a couple of times and she snapped back—that kind of thing." He grinned. "Just normal married behaviour."

"Did she seem frightened of anything in particular?"

"Being burgled."

"But not of her husband?"

Sage shot him a sharp look. "I wouldn't have said so. Hasn't he got an alibi?"

"We've not checked it yet. So there were no undercurrents that struck you, seeing them together?"

"To be honest, Guv, I wasn't looking for any. All that interested me was whether they'd heard anything when the house next door was done."

"Yep. OK. Anything fresh from the neighbours today?"

"Nothing relevant, I'm afraid."

"I suppose it was too much to hope for. Right, Harry, you can knock off now. See you tomorrow. Sally with you?" he added, as Sage turned away.

"We split up to cover more ground, but she'll be back at the car by now."

Webb nodded and went back into the house.


"We've been let off school," Sage reported to Sally, who'd been leaning wearily against the bonnet and straightened as he approached.

"Good; I could do with a quiet evening."

"How about a drink first, to help you unwind?"

"I don't think so, thanks, Skip. I'd rather get home."

"Nonsense, do you the world of good. Anyway," he added with a sly sideways glance as he turned the ignition key, "it's not as though there's anyone waiting for you, is there? I heard on the grapevine you'd split with your feller."

Oh God! Sally thought in a panic; he's not going to start on about Pete, is he? Because, tired as she was, she could easily break down, and then where would she be?

The road was entering the forest, a dark green tunnel where the light filtered patchily through the interwoven branches. Sally, not trusting herself to speak, gripped the edges of her seat tightly.

"Still touchy, are we? Never mind, doll, plenty more fish in the sea, and we're all the same in the dark!"

Sally's teeth fastened in her lip. Please God, don't let him turn off the road. If he tried anything on she'd hit him, which would put her career up the spout. *He was slowing down!* She tensed, then with a wave of thankfulness heard the swish of a car behind them. Impossible to pass on this road, and, since it might well be some of their colleagues following them, turning off was out of the question. The car regained speed and they reached the blessed openness of the main road.

"The offer of a drink still stands," Sage said.

"Not this evening, thanks. Really."

"Suit yourself."

Though weak with relief, Sally was aware that the respite was temporary; he was sure to try again. The sooner Fred Perry returned from sick leave, she thought fervently, the better.

It was without his usual sense of well-being that Ken Jackson opened his front door that evening. Normally he savoured the moment when he put his key in the lock and Millie and the children came running to greet him; but during the last hour, as he and the Governor had walked round the grounds of the Stately Home and looked in at the incident room, he'd been getting more and more anxious about Paul.

"Hello!" he called. "I'm home!"

Millie appeared at the head of the stairs, a finger to her lips. "Hush, love, he's just dropped off."

"Sorry." Jackson went up the stairs two at a time. "How is he?"

"No better, I'm afraid. I took him to the surgery this morning. The doctor said it could be a grumbling appendix."

"Appendicitis, you mean?" Old, doom-laden episodes of "Doctor Findlay's Casebook" flashed through his mind.

"Only grumbling," Millie reassured him. "Which apparently is not much more than an upset tummy. He might have several attacks without their ever coming to anything."

"But can't the doctor give him something?" Jackson was a man of his time, brought up to believe modern science had a cure for everything.

"It seems not. He's to be kept on a liquid diet till he stops being sick, then a very light one for several days. And if the pain gets worse, we're to contact him again."

"That's big of him."

Millie laid her head briefly against his shoulder. "Be fair, love. He's a good doctor."

"I suppose so. Well, since Paul's asleep, where are the others?"

"Vickie's watching TV and the twins are finishing tea. When they got to the biscuit stage I left them for a minute to check up on Paul. We'd better get back, though."

The twins, two months off their second birthday and unaware of the crisis in the household, greeted their parents with wide grins. Both high chairs were covered in a generous coating of chocolate.

"I'm behindhand today," Millie apologized, getting a cloth to one pair of hands while Jackson tackled the other.

"Never mind, I'll bath them. I was afraid I'd be too late."

She brushed the hair off her face with the back of her hand. "Oh, I'm sorry, Ken. I never asked how the day had gone."

"We went waltzing off to the Cotswolds, if you please. A pleasant drive, but not a lot to show for it." He lifted his son out of the chair, holding his head aside to avoid the still-sticky fingers. "I'll tell you about it once we've got this lot to bed." He glanced across at her, catching a rare despondency in her face.

"Don't worry, love," he said rallyingly, holding down his own fears. "He'll be all right."

"Of course he will."

And, reassured that Millie's smile was back in place, Jackson set off for the bathroom.

Alison, ready for bed, lit the night-light she'd bought that morning and set it in its saucer. Stupid, she knew, to need it at her age, and with her husband sleeping beside her. Last night, however, she'd been plagued by nightmares in which it was she who floated in the lily-pond. And now there was talk of murder. She shuddered. At least tonight when her eyes flashed open, uncertain whether she woke or slept, the gentle glow would provide comfort.

She switched off the light and stood for a moment looking at the flickering shadows cast on the ceiling, transported by them back to her childhood. Then, returning to the less happy present, she went to open the window. And it was then, glancing casually down, that she saw the car.

Frowning, Alison pushed up the sash as she had the previous night, leaning out for a better look. But as before, the vehicle was huddled into the corner of the wall beneath her and showed only as a dark hump.

She hesitated. Neil was still dressed and downstairs. Had things been more normal between them, she would have asked him to walk round the corner and have a closer look at it. In the present circumstances, however, it wasn't worth the hassle of facing him again.

She pulled the window down to its accustomed six inches and went to bed.

## CHAPTER 7

On his return home that evening, Webb had called in to see Hannah. Her flat was on the floor below his, looking out over the large gardens which had belonged to the house that originally stood on the site.

As she opened the door to him, her orange cat Pekoe rubbed itself ingratiatingly around his legs. No longer a kitten, it was still a small animal, neat and compact, with a white front and emerald-green eyes.

"Cupboard love!" Webb commented.

"Not at all!" Hannah retorted. "When have you ever fed him? He's merely welcoming you to his domain." She glanced at Webb's face. "You look tired, David. Go and sit down and I'll get you a drink. Have you eaten?"

"A drink will be fine, thanks."

"I said, have you eaten?"

"Look, I'm not on the scrounge. I've a couple of chops upstairs, but I just wanted to relax with you for a few minutes."

"It's goulash and rice this evening," Hannah said carelessly, pouring the drinks. "It'll be ready in fifteen minutes."

He laughed. "Temptress!"

"I saw the six o'clock news; they said that woman at Beckworth had been murdered."

"Yep."

"It's illogical, but it seems much worse when I know the place and was there so recently. I suppose you're working on it?"

"Yes; I've been to see her husband today." Webb took an appreciative sip of his whisky.

"Did he do it?"

He smiled wryly. "If he did, he's not admitting it."

"But could he have done?"

Webb reflected, tilting the golden liquid in his glass. "Yes, I rather think he could. We'll know more tomorrow, when Jackson checks his timing."

"So he wasn't in Beckworth that day?"

"No, he was in Woodstock, and it took him four hours to come home."

*"Four hours!"*

"Says he stopped for a meal, but even so it hardly seems plausible."

"Oh, I don't know; it depends on the restaurant. Sometimes it seems like four hours before they even take your order." She sat opposite him, cradling her glass.

"On a happier note, how was the wedding? I haven't seen you since, though I rang your bell a couple of times."

"I've been at Charlotte's. As you know, I usually go for a few days as soon as we break up, but this time it was postponed because of the wedding." Charlotte Yates, Hannah's aunt, was a lecturer at Oxford. "I only got back this morning. She sends her regards, by the way.

"As to the wedding, it was lovely. Camilla, as you would expect, looked radiant, and Mark was like a dog with two tails. Thank goodness some good came of that sorry business. I hope news of this latest case doesn't reach them on their honeymoon; it would bring it all back." She paused. "Any suspects other than the husband?"

"Nope."

"Ah well, it's early days. Now, I presume you are going to stay for the goulash?"

Webb grinned, and some of his tiredness fell away. "You talked me into it," he said.

Webb was back at the bar of the Green Man, this time in an official capacity. Not having opted for the new licensing hours, the pub was still closed and mine host engaged in wiping down the bar.

"So you weren't only sketching, last time you were here," he commented as Webb produced his warrant card.

"Actually, I was."

"Not looking into the burglary at the same time?"

"No, that wasn't my pigeon. But the murder is."

The landlord shook his head. "Aye, it's a bad business. I was saying how the village had changed, but I never dreamt it had gone that far. Mind, the general feeling is she was killed by a visitor. Rough lot you get sometimes, coming in on those coaches. No reason to suppose it was anyone from the village."

Webb said diplomatically, "I'm sure you've discussed it from every angle. Anyone know anything, would you say?"

The landlord gave a short laugh. "No, but that doesn't stop 'em pontificating. More theories than you could shake a stick at."

"Any that sound feasible?"

"The most popular is that she was having it off with someone and picked the wrong feller. Nothing whatever to back it up, mind, and I wouldn't want to blacken the poor lady's name when she can't stick up for herself."

"Any suggestions for the rôle?"

"We wouldn't know, would we, if he was a visitor."

So village loyalty still existed. Though it might hinder his inquiries, Webb couldn't regret it.

"You've got a point there." He changed tack. "You were saying before that a lot of the young people have moved away." The man nodded. "But there are quite a few still about, I gather?" The Beckworth Bruisers, as Dexter had called them.

"Oh yes, one or two."

"Clients?"

The landlord grimaced. "Yes, and there are times we could do without them. They get a bit wild now and then, which annoys the old brigade, but they're not a bad bunch really."

"They have jobs locally, then?"

"Yes, some work on the estate—gardeners, grooms, odd-job men. Some are farm labourers, some on the dole— and one's following my own trade, down in Shillingham."

"Really? Which pub?"

"The Whistle Stop."

Webb grunted noncommittally. Didn't say much for the lad; the Whistle Stop, which was alongside the station, was in the poorest part of town and there were persistent rumours of drugs changing hands there.

"And all these boys were born and bred here?"

"As far as I know. I remember most of them as young-sters." He paused. "Not figuring them for the job, are you?"

"Not necessarily, but in a murder inquiry we have to check on everyone."

"Well, Mr. Scott could tell you more than I can. He was headmaster of the school till it closed down."

"Ah! Is he still around?"

"Yes—lives at the schoolhouse. The smaller, left-hand half."

"Right, thanks very much for your help, Mr.—?"

"Haydock. Stan Haydock."

"I'll no doubt see you again at lunch-time, on a less formal basis."

"You'll be very welcome, sir."

As Webb reached the corner of the lane, Jackson, who had been to check with the men still working in the grounds, was emerging from a small gate set in the large wrought-iron ones.

"Is that unlocked all the time?" Webb asked, nodding towards it.

"It's not unlocked, Guv. You can let yourself out from the inside, but unless you've a key you have to ring the bell to get in. The lady at the Lodge isn't too happy about run-ning backwards and forwards with our lads going in and out."

"Did you speak to her?"

"Only in passing. Said we'd look in later when her husband's home. About six-thirty, she said." Which meant another fairly late do, he thought, still worrying about Paul.

"It was he who gave a lift to the dead woman," Webb said thoughtfully. "I wonder if his wife knows."

"She soon will. Where now then, Guv?"

Webb nodded across to the schoolhouse on the opposite corner. "A word with the ex-headmaster about his former pupils. Might be quite instructive."

Leslie Scott, who opened the door to them, was a bent, elderly man with bushy eyebrows above rheumy eyes. His hair, still quite plentiful, was snowy white and he wore a neat striped shirt and tie under a beige cardigan. Still very much with it, Webb decided.

"Good morning, sir. I'm sorry to trouble you, but—"

"Been expecting you," Scott said, moving to one side. "Come in, come in. Terrible business."

They followed him into the narrow hallway. The house, which Haydock had referred to as "the smaller half", was in fact only one third of the building, but it was cosy and cheerful and had quite a decent-sized garden, long and narrow, behind it. An elderly woman, hearing their voices, appeared from the direction of the kitchen.

"My wife, Joyce."

Webb shook her hand.

"There's some coffee on the stove," she said. "Could I offer you a cup?"

"That would be welcome. Thank you."

He and Jackson settled themselves as directed on the chintz sofa.

"Now, Mr. Webb," Scott began, "tell us how we can help you. I'm afraid our fingers aren't as much on the pulse as they used to be."

"Did you know Mrs. Dexter, sir?"

"Alas, no. These days, people rush about in their cars instead of walking in the village. Can't blame them; there's nowhere to walk *to*, now the shop's closed."

"You didn't even know her by sight?"

"I couldn't be sure. Believe it or not, I only know our next-door neighbours to nod to—they're out at work all day. As to people farther along the road, they moved into those houses at much the same time, and to be honest I never really sorted out t'other from which. In any case, they have young families and don't want to be bothered with old fogeys like us." His gentle smile took any bitterness from his words.

"Speaking of your next-door neighbours, I hear they were burgled on Tuesday."

The old man pulled down his mouth. "We feel very badly about that. Didn't hear a thing, though you'd think we should have done, through the wall. But this old house is solidly built, none of your flimsy modern stuff, and that dividing wall is part of the original building." He smiled reminiscently. "This room used to be my study, in the old days."

"How long were you headmaster, Mr. Scott?"

"Fifteen years in all, and I worked here for ten before that."

"It must have been a wrench, when the school closed down."

"Nearly broke my heart. Not for myself; I'd reached retiring age and was ready to go. But for the children; all sense of community is lost when they have to travel miles to school. We waged a strong campaign to keep it open, but in the end we were beaten."

"I suppose there are quite a few of your former pupils about the place?"

"Yes, and that's heart-breaking too. The brighter ones have done well for themselves, as you'd expect, but the below-average have been badly served. Few jobs are going hereabouts, and a lot of them are wasting their lives drifting from one poorly paid post to another. If, indeed, they can find work at all."

"I know this is a difficult question, but I'd be grateful

for your frankness." Webb paused, wondering how best to phrase it. "Were there any among them who might have developed—criminal tendencies?"

"Oh dear. I do hope we're not talking about the murder?"

"There are also the burglaries to consider," Webb said obliquely. "I hear some of them are given to hanging round on street corners. They'd have a good idea when a house was empty."

"As to that, I couldn't say. We do have the occasional spot of trouble; a fight broke out one night last week, I believe, between some of our boys and a crowd from the camping site. Joe Barlow was telling me he had to break it up."

"Joe Barlow?" The surname rang a bell: a Mrs. Barlow had been one of those who found the body.

"Our milkman. He lives down Tinker's Lane. In fact, his son is one of those I'm concerned about, though he has a job of sorts, in a public house in Shillingham."

"Then why are you concerned?"

The old man met Webb's eye. "We are talking confidentially, I take it?"

"Of course."

"Well, he was never a boy I felt I could trust. Caught cheating and so on. He had a chip on his shoulder, I don't know why, and since he's a strong character the other boys followed his lead."

"A gang leader, in fact?"

"I shouldn't put it as strongly as that, Chief Inspector. But I have to say that if there was trouble, Darren Barlow would be the first I'd ask about it."

"Does he still live at home?"

"No; for one thing, the house isn't big enough. It already has to accommodate Joe's crippled father and the married daughter and her husband. But he was home over Easter; I saw him nearly run down Mr. Parrish on his motorbike."

From the corner of his eye, Webb watched Jackson write down Darren's name. "Who are the other boys he's friendly with?"

The old man mentioned four or five, who were also noted. He remembered most of their addresses, too, which Webb thought pretty good going. Harry Sage could follow them up.

"Right; we're most grateful for your help, Mr. Scott. If you remember anything else, perhaps you would contact us."

Webb stood for a moment on the pavement outside the schoolhouse to get his bearings. The building was at the crossroads of the village; leading up to the right was the road to the church which he'd followed on his sketching trip, and just across it, most conveniently placed, the village hall-cum-incident room, with the mobile police canteen parked outside. Opposite them lay Tinker's Lane with the estate gates on the right-hand corner and the Green Man some fifty yards down on the left. Between himself and the lane the main road ran through the village. A pity the old man wasn't given to standing at his windows; if he had been, there'd be little he'd miss.

Webb glanced at his watch. Just after eleven. "What time do milkmen get home, Ken?"

"Depends on the round, I should think, Guv."

"Well, we need to speak to his wife anyway; Sage only took a preliminary statement. Number 17, I think it was. Might even get a few snippets on young Darren while we're there."

Together they walked down the lane, glancing appreciatively at the pretty little houses that lined it, with their steep roofs and gabled windows and the white picket fences that edged the minute front gardens. On the other side of the road the high wall of the estate kept pace with them, with the wide empty space of the visitors' car-park at its foot.

A clip-clopping of hooves preceded a procession of six horses, each mounted by a small girl in jodhpurs and hard hat. As they trotted sedately past, the one in front solemnly raised her crop in greeting. There was a livery stable on the lower road, Webb remembered, watching the beautifully groomed animals disappearing down the hill.

Jackson was slowing, as Webb had known he would, to read the menu displayed outside the Green Man. Webb, maintaining his pace, said over his shoulder, "They do a formidable sausage, Ken. You'll have earned it by the time we get back here." His sergeant's capacity for food was a never-ending source of wonder, but he conceded that without Ken's need for regular sustenance he himself might well have succumbed to ulcers before now.

Number 17 was no different from its neighbours except that a bus stop was positioned in front of it. Jackson pushed open the gate and they went up the short path to the door.

Mrs. Barlow could best be described as bonny, Webb decided; rounded without being unduly plump, with a pleasant, fresh-complexioned face and greying brown hair.

"I've already spoken to the police," she said in her soft Broadshire burr, her eyes showing alarm at this second visit.

"I appreciate that, ma'am, but we've a few more questions, if you could spare us a couple of minutes."

From the hall behind her came a querulous old voice. "Who's that, Hazel? Not the ruddy cops again?"

"Hush, Dad." Mrs. Barlow, flushing, shot them an apologetic glance. "Come in if you'd like to. I'm afraid we're rather cluttered."

She spoke no more than the truth. Pretty the cottage might be, but it was not designed for family living. As they walked past the open door on their left, Webb, with a sideways glance, caught sight of an old man in a wheelchair glowering out at him. His occupancy of that room explained the congested kitchen into which they were now shown. Though of reasonable size, it seemingly doubled as living-room, since there was a sofa, two armchairs and a television taking up space that could ill be spared. Mrs. Barlow swept up some newspapers to clear a space for them to sit down.

"Is your father-in-law able to get about much?" Webb asked, watching her.

"Oh, certainly. He zooms round all over the village."

"So he's fairly independent, then?"

"Yes, and his job on the gate helps." As Webb looked back at her uncomprehendingly, she added, "He issues tickets up at the House on Open Days."

"Does he indeed?" Webb's casual air disappeared. "Was he there on Monday?"

She nodded. "All afternoon. Now, sir, how can I help you?"

He'd see the old man on the way out. "Could you begin by explaining how you came to find Mrs. Dexter?"

"Oh." She perched on the edge of the table, clasping her hands tightly. "Well, I work in the greenhouses up at the House, growing flowers for the private apartments and various functions that are held there. But when we have a really big occasion, like the wedding last Saturday, professional arrangers come in, bringing the fancy flowers with them. We settle their bill and include their charges in our account to the clients. Saves them having a lot of separate bills, you see."

"Yes?" said Webb encouragingly, mystified as to the relevancy of all this.

"Well, sir, I remembered I hadn't passed the arrangers' bill on to Mrs. Carey, so I took it up on Wednesday morning. And I was just leaving when Mrs. Cummings came round."

"And why exactly did Mrs. Cummings call?" No harm in getting a corroborative statement.

"Because she'd just heard Mrs. Dexter was missing, and

remembered seeing her in the grounds on Monday afternoon."

"Had you met Mrs. Cummings before?"

"No, sir. Neither of us had."

"What about Mrs. Dexter?"

"I'd seen her once or twice in her car, but I didn't know her name."

"So how did you set about looking for her?"

Hazel explained how they'd separated, and her own fruitless search of the walled garden. "I met Mrs. Cummings coming back from the rose-garden, and she'd not had any luck either. We'd arranged to meet again in front of the House, but when Mrs. Carey didn't come, we went to the pond to look for her."

"And when you saw Mrs. Dexter in the water, you recognized her?"

Hazel nodded and bent her head.

"Had you been in the grounds yourself on Monday, Mrs. Barlow?"

"Only on the way to the Orangery. My daughter and I were helping with the teas."

"What time would that have been?"

"From three till five-thirty. Mavis didn't stay all the time, because she's expecting and can't stand for long periods."

"Now you know who Mrs. Dexter was, did she come in for a cup of tea?"

"No, sir."

"And you didn't see her at any time during the afternoon?"

"No."

"When you'd seen her about the village, had she ever been with anyone other than her children?"

"Only the once, sir, with Mr. Carey."

"When was that?" If the time differed from what Dexter had said, it might point to more than one assignation. But his hopes were dashed.

"The afternoon of the wedding. Last Saturday, that is. They drove past when I was weeding at the front."

There was a pause, and Hazel said nervously, "Could I get you some tea or something?"

"No, thank you; we've just had coffee with Mr. Scott."

As though glad to change the subject, she said eagerly, "He's a lovely old gentleman, isn't he?"

"Very pleasant. He was saying your husband had to break up a fight between some youths last week."

"That's right. It was that lot from down the road that started it. There's often trouble during the holiday season when the campers come."

"Lucky your husband happened to be around. What time does he get home, by the way? I'd like to ask him about it."

"Well, as it happens he's home now, sir. He hasn't been too well the last couple of days."

"I'm sorry. Is he in bed?"

"Yes. Dr. Charles says there's a bug going round. But I'm sure he'd come down, if you want to see him."

"If he's up to it, I'd be grateful."

She excused herself and they heard her running upstairs and voices from the room above. Then came the squeak of springs, a thud as feet reached the floor, and a creak of boards.

"Not a lot of privacy, is there, Guv?" Jackson said in a low voice.

"No; it must be pretty trying."

Joe Barlow appeared at the door in a red plaid dressing-gown, a bear of a man with shaggy hair. Webb had the impression he was usually ruddy-faced, but now his cheeks were pale.

"I'm sorry to drag you from your bed, Mr. Barlow," h said, rising.

"That's all right, sir." Moving slowly across the roo Barlow seated himself on one of the upright chairs at

table, from where he eyed Webb a trifle warily. "What can I do for you?"

"I was hearing about the fight the other evening, and wondered if any of those involved could have had anything to do with the burglaries. I presume you know them all?"

"The village lads, of course, but not the campers."

"When did the caravans arrive?" Webb remembered seeing them on Saturday.

"The day of the fight, the first of them. There's always trouble when they come, rivalry, you might say."

"I believe you have a son of your own about that age?"

Mrs. Barlow drew in her breath and her husband flushed. "Yes, but he wasn't involved. He's living in Shillingham now."

"The local lads will be his friends, though?"

The man nodded. "Word has it there've been other robberies round about."

"That's true."

"Well, our lads wouldn't go far afield. I doubt you'll find the culprits here."

He might find a murderer, though.

"The gentleman was asking about Mrs. Dexter, Joe," murmured his wife.

"Did you know her, Mr. Barlow?"

"In a manner of speaking. I delivered her milk and helped out now and then in the garden."

"Were you aware of any stress between her and her husband?"

Joe shook his head. "I never saw them together; he was always at work when I was up there."

"Ever see her with anyone else?"

"No. She seemed to keep herself to herself, if you know what I mean."

There seemed little more the man could tell him, and he was obviously tiring. Webb said, "Thank you for your help, Mr. Barlow. We won't keep you out of bed any longer, but we'd be grateful for a word with your father."

They were led back along the passage to the small, stuffy room the old man inhabited. He sat like a wizened spider in his wheelchair, glaring up at them. "Well? What is it, then?"

"I understand, sir, that you work on the gate up at the estate?"

"What if I do? Nothing wrong with that, is there?"

"I wonder if you happened to notice Mrs. Dexter going through on Monday afternoon?"

"Young man, have you any idea how many tickets I issued on Monday? Six hundred and fifty-seven. I was that busy I wouldn't have noticed my own mother."

Webb, who hadn't been addressed as "young man" for more years than he cared to remember, murmured an apology. "Did you know the lady, sir?"

"Used to see her flashing round in her fancy motor."

"Was she ever with anyone?"

"Only her kids. Who else did you expect—the Queen of Sheba?"

Webb and Jackson exchanged glances. "We won't bother you any further then, sir." And meekly they allowed Hazel Barlow to show them out.

# CHAPTER 8

The Cummings family were in their front garden when Webb and Jackson arrived. The two boys, pleasant-looking youngsters of about fourteen and sixteen, were sent round the back with the dog while their parents led the policemen inside.

Not much indication that this was a former cowshed-cum-stable, Jackson thought, noting the highly polished beams and the Chinese rugs on the floor.

"On holiday, are you, sir?" Webb was asking Mr. Cummings.

"Yes, I've taken a couple of weeks while the boys are off school." He paused. "Any news on the burglary?"

"Not as yet, I'm afraid." Webb turned to the woman. She was small and dark with short wavy hair and brown eyes, and was now watching him with apprehension.

"I suppose it's me you've come to see," she said jerkily. "But I told the other man all I know."

"I'm sorry, Mrs. Cummings; I know it's a nuisance to have to go through everything again but it is necessary, especially since we now know we're dealing with murder."

She flushed. "Of course. How selfish of me."

Led by his questions, she told a story which dovetailed neatly with Hazel Barlow's.

"I'd spoken to Dexter as he left for work," Bob Cummings put in. "The poor devil was in a frightful state, and I gathered your lot hadn't been too helpful."

"Missing-person cases are tricky, sir. If an adult wishes to disappear, it's not up to us to track them down, however much their family wants them back. And she *had* taken a coat and handbag with her, which made it appear voluntary."

"I see your point. Where is Dexter, by the way? I called round last night to invite him to supper, but there was no one there."

"He's moved back to London for the moment. Staying with friends."

"Best thing, I suppose. Poor devil," he added again.

"Gina!" called a voice from the hall.

Bob Cummings rose swiftly and moved to the door, but he was too late. An elderly woman had pushed it open and stood staring at the assembled company.

"These are the police, Ma, come to see Gina about Mrs. Dexter. My mother-in-law, Mrs. Irving."

"Well, I hope to goodness you're going to do something about all this," Mrs. Irving said severely, fixing them with a steely gaze. "We've been here just over a week and suffered robbery, murder, fights outside the house and wilful damage to our property, and I for one am not prepared to put up with it."

"Mother—please!" Gina Cummings also rose.

"It's not as though I wanted to come here in the first place. I did tell you, Gina, that I thought it extravagant and unnecessary to buy this house when you've a perfectly good one in London. If you want a second home, I said, why not choose one where it's warm and sunny and there's a good class of people about? The South of France, for example."

Webb, feeling his way through this tirade, extracted something that had interested him.

"You spoke of wilful damage, madam. Was this apart from the burglary?"

"Yes, there was some obscene graffiti on our front door."

"Oh Mother, really! It wasn't obscene and no damage was done. It washed off."

"Eventually," she conceded with a sniff.

Remembering the faded circle on the door of the Dexters' house, Webb's interest deepened. "What exactly was it, ma'am?"

"Only a face," Gina said. "Some children probably drew it."

"There was nothing childish about it," Mrs. Irving maintained. "It had a disgustingly hideous leer."

"How was it executed?" Webb asked her daughter. "Chalk?"

"No, green felt pen."

"And when did you discover it?"

"When we arrived a week last Wednesday to find the house broken into. I suppose the burglars might have done it; I never thought of that."

"Did you mention it to the officers who came about the burglary?"

"No, I didn't think it important." She hesitated, anxiously noting Webb's frown. "It isn't, is it?"

"I'm not sure, Mrs. Cummings. But I suspect that the Dexters had a similar experience."

"And look what happened to them!" exclaimed Mrs. Irving triumphantly. "I *said* you should have told the police, but then no one takes any notice of me."

"Can you describe the face, Mrs. Cummings?"

Gina shrugged. "Tight curly hair, a squint, I think, and a tongue sticking out. Not pleasant, I grant you."

"You haven't heard of anyone else acquiring one?"

"Actually, Chief Inspector, we hardly know anyone here, and it's not a thing you'd mention casually in the street, is it?"

"You didn't speak of it to Mrs. Dexter, for example?"

She shook her head.

"To come back to Easter Monday, then. What time did you go to Beckworth House?"

"About three, I suppose. We'd seen cars and coaches streaming past, and thought it might be interesting to look round."

Webb turned to Mrs. Irving. "Did you go as well, ma'am?"

"No, I didn't, thank heaven, or I might have ended up with my throat cut, too."

Forbearing from pointing out that no one had had their throat cut, Webb turned back to Gina. "And can you tell me again how you came to see Mrs. Dexter?"

Patiently she repeated what she'd told Alison Carey and, later, Sergeant Sage.

"So she was standing at the top of the drive, but you didn't notice what direction she took after that?"

"That's right. Though even if I had, it wouldn't have occurred to us to go after her. After all, we hardly knew her."

It was a constant refrain in this village, Webb thought

irritably. "You might have noticed if someone had followed her, though," he pointed out sharply.

"Oh, I see. Well, I'm sorry, but I didn't."

"What made you think, when you heard she was missing, that she might still be in the grounds?"

"Well, Mr. Dexter and the children had left mid-morning, and I reasoned that if she'd intended going away, she'd have gone soon after they did. It was at least six hours later that I saw her, which seemed odd. So I thought I ought to do something."

A somewhat belated twinge of neighbourliness, Webb reflected sourly as he prepared to take his leave.

"Lunch, Guv?" Jackson queried hopefully when they were back on the pavement.

"Yes, I reckon so. We're meeting Sage and Pierce for a briefing at two; I want them to interview the people at the campsite."

The Green Man was well patronized, but the buzz of conversation faltered as they entered the public bar, though the landlord greeted them cheerfully. After placing their orders they retreated to a window table with their beer, and gradually the volume of sound regained its previous level.

"And the Swindon restaurant wasn't much help on Dexter?" Webb recapped, wiping the foam from his mouth. Real ale, he thought appreciatively.

"Not really. They were fairly hectic on Monday and not prepared to estimate the length of time any one person might have taken over his meal." He grinned. "Probably thought we were from Egon Ronay investigating a complaint!"

"Which means it's still possible he could have nipped back, done the dirty deed, then made himself scarce and arrived home openly much later."

"Be a bit risky though, wouldn't it? I mean, Mrs. Cummings saw his wife; she might easily have seen him too. Added to which, he didn't know his missis was going to the gardens."

"We've only his word for that."

Their number was called and Jackson went to the bar to collect their sausages.

"When we've finished eating," Webb said with his mouth full, "I'd like you to ring through to Carrington Street and get them to check up on young Barlow; it's quite possible he's got a record."

Jackson grunted acknowledgement. He'd take the chance to phone home as well; Paul had still been asleep when he left for work.

"And we must get on to house-to-house. I want to find out if anyone else had drawings on their doors."

Jackson stopped chewing and looked at him in surprise. "You're taking that seriously, Guv?"

"I'm not sure. I've got an odd feeling about it, I don't know why. Anyway, we've little enough to go on; we can't risk overlooking what we have."

Hazel said, "We had another visit from the police this morning. A different pair this time."

Alison nodded absently. "Yes, they wanted to know what time my husband gets home."

Hazel flushed. "I hope I haven't got Mr. Carey into trouble, saying I saw him with Mrs. Dexter."

"He was only giving her a lift," Alison said lightly, keeping her eyes on the computer screen. "I doubt if they'll be after him for that. They're probably hoping she said something that might give them a clue."

"Yes, of course." Hazel breathed a sigh of relief, watching as Alison punched the keyboard and studied the figures on the screen. "You make that look so easy," she added admiringly. "It would frighten me to death—and to think I had the nerve to apply for your job!"

"You did?" Alison turned in surprise. "I never knew that."

"Oh, I hadn't a hope really. But the money would have

been useful, and if we could have had the Lodge, it would have left more room at Number Seventeen."

"Sorry about that!"

Hazel laughed. "Don't be; even if you hadn't got it, I'd have been a long way down the list. Well, I must stop wasting your time and get up to the greenhouses." She paused at the door of the little office. "Do you think we'll be opening tomorrow? Dad was asking."

"I don't see why not. They seem to have finished in the gardens."

Hazel shuddered. "I'll never go near that lily-pond again."

"Lucky we didn't find her in the greenhouse, then!"

When Hazel had gone, Alison's thoughts returned to Neil. *Had* he been hoping to start a liaison with Carol Dexter? Why else had he failed to mention he'd spent an afternoon with her? Restlessly she stood up and moved to the window. She felt unsettled, threatened, ill-at-ease. Hardly surprising, when there was a murderer at large. But the killer would be miles away by now; he was hardly likely to hang around when the village was full of police.

Of course! she thought suddenly; that car she'd seen from her window must belong to the police! It was such an obvious solution she was surprised it hadn't occurred to her before. They probably kept a team of men in the village overnight.

The extent of her relief was an indication of how much the car's presence had disturbed her. If only all her other problems could be so easily resolved, she thought wistfully as she returned to her work.

The campsite halfway down the hill was filled to capacity. At least two dozen caravans lined the perimeter in what seemed to Sally uncomfortable proximity, and since it was early afternoon, the smell of several dozen lunches still hung in the air. In a far corner three dogs were chasing each other, barking shrilly, and transistor radios vied with each other for prominence.

Surveying the pandemonium, Sage mentally went over Webb's instructions. "There are various things we want to know, Harry. First, whether any of them went up to the opening of Beckworth House, and if so, details of times, etcetera. Second—though they're not likely to volunteer the information—who was involved in the fight last week. If no names are forthcoming, take a note of the most likely participants. Third, how many kids there are aged ten and over, whether any of them have been up in the village unaccompanied, and how many have felt pens."

"If you're on about the drawing, Guv," Ken Jackson had interrupted, "the Cummingses found it when they arrived on the twenty-second, and according to Barlow the first campers only got there that day."

"Nevertheless, we might as well rule it out officially. And if any of the families are regulars, Harry, probe around and see if any specific enmity exists between their lads and those in the village."

All of which could keep them going till the middle of next week, Sage thought glumly.

"Well, Skip," Sally prompted at his side, "where do we start?"

"You take the left side and I'll take the right. Last one home's a sissy."

It was slow and not very rewarding work. The campers were understandably jumpy about the murder and, however innocent, reluctant to volunteer anything that could link them with Beckworth. Two families had already cut short their holiday and returned home, and clearly some of those remaining were now wishing they'd done likewise. Sage noted without comment the names of those who'd departed.

Sally, possibly because of her ingenuous manner, was meeting with less resistance. Under the influence of her smile, several families admitted to having visited the

Stately Home on Monday, though a description of Carol Dexter rang no bells with them. She also uncovered a number of last week's pugilists, some of whom would have been hard put to deny their participation since they still sported cut lips and black eyes.

"Think they own the place, that village mob," one youth said indignantly. "All we were trying to do was have a peaceful drink, but they wouldn't leave us alone." Which, naturally, was the direct opposite of what they'd been told in Beckworth.

"You were heard to say you'd go back and sort them out," Sally reminded him.

"We might, at that," he muttered rebelliously.

"Oh no you won't, my lad!" put in his mother. "They've got more important things to do up there than worry about you lot. You can do your drinking in Lethbridge or Shillingham from now on."

On the felt-pen topic Sally suffered an *embarras de richesse.* Every family with young children, which was about seventy-five percent of them, admitted to possessing sets of the pens; it seemed they were an essential provision on camping holidays, in case of wet weather. Green ones were included among every other colour, but mothers insisted that the children had never been as far as the village unaccompanied. Whether their big brothers had pocketed a pen or two was anybody's guess. Frankly, Sally couldn't see that it mattered. Kids scribbled on any available surface—it was a fact of life. If it was on someone else's property they deserved a smacked bottom but not, surely, police interrogation. Still, no doubt the Governor knew what he was doing; he usually did. Slowly and methodically, she continued with her task.

Jackson's lunch-time phone-calls had established that Darren Barlow had twice been convicted of petty larceny, and that his son Paul was slightly better—the latter item being to his mind much the more important. All the same, he'd be glad when he could go home and check for himself. Which, he reflected, as he and Webb stood on the doorstep of the Lodge, shouldn't be too long now.

They had timed their arrival to give them half an hour with Mrs. Carey before her husband was due home. The stone house nestled just inside the estate walls but had a minute front garden of its own and a somewhat larger back one, screened from prying eyes by a high hedge.

Webb ducked his head as they were shown into the sitting-room. It was as small and prettily furnished as a doll's house and he felt large and out of place, nervous that he might inadvertently knock something over.

Mrs. Carey was a handsome woman with bright chestnut hair and hazel eyes, and she had greeted them calmly enough. But there was an undeniable sense of strain about her, and Webb wondered if this was solely due to having discovered the woman's body.

"Were you home yourself on Easter Monday, Mrs. Carey?" he inquired, settling himself cautiously on a spindly-legged chair.

"No, we went to a point-to-point at Chipping Claydon."

"Getting home at what time?"

She shrugged. "Soon after six, I suppose."

"By which time the main gates were locked?"

"Oh yes, but that doesn't concern us; we garage the cars behind the Green Man."

"And you'll have a key to the small gate?"

"That's right. There are other entrances to the estate, of course, for tradesmen and estate workers, but when they're unlocked they're under constant supervision. There are priceless treasures up at the House, and the insurers insist on maximum security."

"Very wise," said Webb drily. His question was academic. Had Carol Dexter been alive when the main gates closed, she would already have left. Therefore her killer, whether her husband or anyone else, must have entered in the normal way during public admission. Unless he was already on the estate.

For the third time he went through the details of finding the body, and again they tallied closely with what he'd heard before.

"You didn't know Mrs. Dexter yourself?" So Hazel Barlow had led him to believe.

"No. I regret now that I never contacted her."

"But I gather your husband had met her?"

A quick, sharp glance from those hazel eyes. "He gave her a lift once, when her car broke down."

"Which was only a couple of days before her death?"

Alison nodded, avoiding his eyes. Something was worrying her, Webb thought. And Dexter had hinted that his wife's interest in the House stemmed from her meeting with Carey. Still, if the man had been at the point-to-point—

"I gather you're booking manager here, ma'am?"

"That's right."

"So you must know the grounds pretty well?"

"Yes, though I'm mainly involved with the House."

"But surely you walk round the garden fairly regularly?"

"It's a private house, Chief Inspector. Unless I'm on business, I respect that privacy."

Which put him in his place. "Did business take you into the grounds on Tuesday?"

"No."

"If you hadn't specifically searched for Mrs. Dexter, how long might it have been before she was found?"

She shrugged. "The gardeners go round before an Open Day, tidying up generally. But they didn't notice her on Tuesday and they probably wouldn't have today." She paused. "We are allowed to open tomorrow?"

"Yes, that's been cleared."

She nodded. "Anyway, by this time she might have— floated out to the middle, or sunk—" She broke off with a shudder. "I don't know, thank God, what happens in such cases, but I'd say there's a good chance she'd never have been found."

Before he could answer they heard the front door open, and a minute later Neil Carey came into the room. He was a tall man with mid-brown wavy hair, a lean, intelligent face and slate-grey eyes.

"I was expecting you," he said shortly, as his wife performed the introductions.

Webb said smoothly, "You have the distinction, sir, of being almost the only person in the village to have spoken to Mrs. Dexter."

A quick look at his wife. Was he wondering what she'd told them? "That's right. Her car was out of action and she had some urgent shopping to do. I was at a loose end, so I ran her to Lethbridge."

"Which would have given you the chance for quite a long chat?"

"Yes. We discovered a mutual dislike of Beckworth."

Alison Carey moved protestingly and Webb, taking up the cue, said, "You don't like living here?"

"No. I find the house cramped, the village unfriendly and the distance from work inconvenient."

There was a brief, embarrassed pause. Then his wife said, "We came here when I was offered this job, Chief Inspector. My husband was—out of work at the time, and we were glad to get it." It was, she realized, the first time she hadn't used the word "redundant", which had always been an unconscious lie.

"You've found another position now?" Webb was concentrating on the man.

"Yes, in Reading. We've been discussing the possibility of moving nearer."

"And Mrs. Dexter also found Beckworth unfriendly?" From what he'd seen of it, he wasn't surprised.

"Yes, she was quite strung up about it. She seemed to feel—vulnerable."

"After the first burglary, you mean?"

"That was one thing. Then there was the graffito on her door, though I was able to reassure her on that."

Webb's sudden movement took Jackson by surprise and he dropped his notebook. He stooped quickly and retrieved it.

"Tell me about the graffito."

Carey looked surprised. "Oh, it was nothing. Just a face some vandal had drawn. But it really upset her—out of all proportion, I thought. Still, she calmed down when I told her we'd had one."

"You had a face drawn on your door?"

"That's right. A couple of weeks ago."

"Can you describe it?"

"Like a gargoyle, really. Snake-like hair and tongue sticking out."

"Did you see it, Mrs. Carey?"

"No, Neil only mentioned it after he'd washed it off."

"And Mrs. Dexter was reassured to know you'd had one?"

"Yes, she'd thought it was something personal. She said, 'Then my husband was right, it was just a yob with a felt pen going round the village.' "

"The people at Mews Grange had one as well," Webb said.

"Really? There must have been a plague of them."

"That doesn't worry you, Mr. Carey?"

"*Worry* me? No, why on earth should it?"

"Because in the two other instances we know of, one was followed by burglary and the other by murder."

"My God, you're not saying there's a connection?"

"No, I'm not. But I'm saying there might be. We certainly have to find out who's been going round daubing front doors, and why." He paused, wondering how to frame his next question without upsetting Carey's wife.

"When you left Mrs. Dexter last Saturday, did you make any arrangements to meet again?"

To his surprise, the man flushed darkly. "No, I did not, why should I?"

"Well, you knew she was lonely, and you had something in common in your dislike of the village." Another pause. "It occurred to me that you might have suggested she come to see the House and gardens on Monday, but your wife tells me you were out."

Some quality in the sudden silence made Webb glance quickly from husband to wife. He was staring at her, she at the floor. Webb said sharply, "You *were* out, weren't you, Mr. Carey? At the point-to-point?"

"No, Chief Inspector, as it happens I wasn't. My wife and daughter went but I didn't."

Jackson, pencil poised, sat motionless.

"Then *did* you arrange to meet Mrs. Dexter in the grounds, sir?"

"No, I most definitely did not."

"Did you perhaps bump into her by accident?"

"*No,* damn it!"

"Can you tell me, then, how you spent the day?"

"My wife had left some trays of bedding plants for me to attend to. That took all morning, then I had lunch and watched bank-holiday sport on television."

"You didn't go into the grounds at all?"

"I did not. As my wife will bear out, I intensely dislike the House being open to the public. Humanity in the mass is to be avoided at all costs."

"Is there anyone who can confirm that you didn't leave the house, sir?"

"Since I didn't see anybody, I doubt it. Old Bert Barlow was on the gate, but he was far too busy to notice my movements, even if he'd been interested in them. Had I known the poor woman was going to get killed," he added venomously, "I should, of course, have been careful to arrange an alibi."

Ignoring the jibe, Webb said mildly, "Did Mrs. Dexter mention anything else that upset her?"

"The village boys played her up, making remarks as she passed. That kind of thing."

"Nothing more specific?"

"Not that I remember."

"Well, if anything should come back to you, I'd be grateful to hear of it. In the meantime we'll leave you to your evening meal. Thanks for your help."

Back outside the gates, Jackson said, "I thought you were going to nab him then and there, Guv!"

"On what grounds, Ken? What possible motive could he have? If he did fancy her, he wouldn't be likely to bump her off when he'd just established contact."

"Unless she wouldn't play ball and threatened to tell his wife."

"He doesn't seem the type to kill to keep a bit of hanky-panky quiet. If he *is* our man, we'll have to dig deeper to find a motive. But not tonight. Time we knocked off. It's been a long day."

# CHAPTER 9

At Beckworth House that Saturday there was a team of uniformed policemen in the car-park and two plainclothes men alongside Bert Barlow's kiosk.

Though logically it was unlikely that visitors who'd been there on Monday would return so soon, Webb was student enough of human nature to take the ghoul factor into account. The type of person who slowed down on motorways the better to stare at an accident was more than likely to beat a path back to Beckworth House, whether they'd already been there that week or not. So DCs Marshbanks and Finch, holding photographs of Carol Dexter, spent their afternoon asking the same two questions: "Were you here on Monday?" and, if answered in the affir-

mative, "Did you see this woman?" Should the reply to
that also prove positive, they were to bleep the incident
room and someone would be sent to assist in the questioning.

In the car-park, the task of the uniformed men was
equally repetitive. Quite a few of the coach drivers had
been over on bank holiday, but when asked if on the return
trip there had been a shortfall in numbers—or, indeed, a
surplus—or if anyone boarding had appeared wet, dishev-
elled or generally upset, they disclaimed any knowledge of
their passengers. It appeared the organizations in charge of
the various outings had been responsible for checking
numbers, and they had already been contacted as a matter
of routine.

Webb sat in the village hall-cum-incident room drinking coffee and staring morosely at the blank wall of the
estate across the road. Teams had now visited every house
in the village, and from the mounds of information still to
be sifted he'd extracted the fact that the front doors of five
of them had been defaced with green ink. Three he'd been
aware of: Coppins Farmhouse, Mews Grange and
Beckworth Lodge. Of the others, Number 2 The Schoolhouse, he noted grimly, had also been the victim of a burglary. The remaining house was one of the luxury retirement bungalows.

Furthermore, the instances had been spread over several
weeks. The Careys had repeated their original estimate of
"a couple of weeks ago", which was echoed by the Parrishes. On the other hand, the retired couple in the bungalow were quite definite that their graffito had appeared at
the beginning of the month, and the Cummingses had discovered theirs when they arrived in Beckworth just before
Easter. Though it might, of course, have been there some
time. The only one they hadn't been able to check on was
the most important—that at the Dexters' house.

Frowningly Webb studied the map of the village pinned
on the wall. The Schoolhouse, Coppins and Mews Grange

were all in a row next to each other, the bungalow faced Coppins across the main road, and the Lodge was diagonally opposite the school. Very cosy. But why had the other section of the Schoolhouse escaped attention? A leftover fear of "the Beak"? That might reinforce the Bruisers theory.

What he found more disturbing was the serious consequences that had befallen three of the five marked houses. Again, why? And was there a connection? The possibility that the graffiti had been an advance guide to the burglars didn't even merit consideration. Visiting the area twice would have doubled the risk for the thieves, and even more obviously, the occupants were not likely to leave such vandalism unexpunged.

There was nothing for it but to go and see the people concerned and ask if anything else unusual had occurred.

He pulled a file towards him and, flicking it open, ran through both Sage's and the house-to-house interviews with the Parrishes. Giles Parrish had admitted "strolling over the road" to Beckworth House on Monday, but not to seeing Carol Dexter there. The drawing, Webb noted, had not been mentioned at either interview and emerged only in response to a direct question later. Perhaps, like Neil Carey, they'd attached no importance to it. But Mrs. Dexter had. Again, why? Did she know or suspect more than the others did about the source of the drawing? And was that why she died?

Collecting Ken Jackson on his way out, Webb crossed Church Lane and turned into the second gateway of the Schoolhouse.

Giles Parrish appeared round the side of the house in answer to their ring and, after Webb identified himself, led the way to the back garden where his wife, resplendent in lime-green trousers, was kneeling in front of a flowerbed with a tray of seedlings beside her. She scrambled to her feet and came towards them, brushing the soil from her hands. An odd-looking woman, Jackson thought; her plume of orange hair and the vivid trousers made her look like a rather bedraggled parrot.

"How can we help you, Chief Inspector?" Parrish inquired, waving them towards a garden bench. "I suppose it's too much to hope there's been any development on the burglary?"

"Not as yet, sir. You informed an officer making a routine check that you'd found some graffiti on your door."

Parrish frowned. "Why all the interest? It wasn't anything serious."

"Have you any idea who might have done it?"

"Oh, the young louts that hang around here, I should think. A ne'er-do-well bunch if ever I saw one."

"Are you aware of doing anything to antagonize them?"

"Only existing and being relatively successful. There's a creed of envy nowadays, Inspector, a longing to see those better off than yourself brought low. Not a pleasant attitude, but unfortunately pretty universal." He paused. "How did you hear of it, anyway? We didn't report it."

"You weren't the only recipients, sir. There were four other instances."

"Well, in a selfish way that's quite a relief. Means we haven't been singled out, if you know what I mean. Who else had them?"

"The people at the Lodge, Mews Grange, one of the bungalows—and your next-door neighbours." He nodded towards the fence dividing the garden from that of the Dexters.

"And one of them reported it?"

"No, but it came out during an interview." Webb paused, and added deliberately, "In connection with Mrs. Dexter's death."

Parrish sobered. "That was a god-awful thing, wasn't it?"

"Did you know her, sir?" He asked the question almost casually, expecting the standard Beckworth reply. But to his surprise Parrish replied, "We exchanged the odd word on a couple of occasions."

"When was the last time?"

"About two weeks ago, I suppose. We arrived at our respective gates at the same time and made the odd comment as one does. In fact—I'd forgotten all about it—she asked if we'd one of those devices for aerating the lawn and I said I'd look it out for her."

"And you're quite sure you didn't catch even a glimpse of her on bank-holiday Monday?"

"Absolutely certain."

"So that meeting at the gate was the last sight or sound you had of her?"

He intercepted an exchanged look between husband and wife, and at his raised eyebrows Mrs. Parrish flushed slightly.

"We did overhear them—talking—one evening," she said unwillingly.

"Talking?"

"Having a row, actually," Giles Parrish said briskly. "It quite surprised us, they'd always been so quiet before."

Webb let his breath out in a long sigh. "And when was this?"

"The day that young fool nearly ran into me on his bike. Last weekend, it must have been."

"Can you be more exact, sir? It might be important."

"Saturday, then. Yes, that's right, Saturday evening."

"And did you gather what the row was about?"

Parrish moved uncomfortably. "Look, Chief Inspector, the poor man's suffered enough, surely, without dragging all this up."

"We'll use our discretion," Webb said ambiguously.

"In any case I don't really remember. I know Carey's running her into Lethbridge came into it."

"She said she should have known no one here could be trusted," Lalage put in. "And that she'd been glad of someone to talk to."

"Meaning Mr. Carey, presumably."

She creased her brow. "No, I don't think so; he hadn't been mentioned at that stage."

"Then what did she say about him?"

"Only that his giving her a lift was her husband's fault, because he wouldn't take her himself."

So Stewart and Carol Dexter had had a row two days before her death, which made the question of his meal in Swindon even more crucial. Webb had dispatched a couple of DCs to drive from Woodstock to Swindon and from Swindon to Beckworth along the route taken by Dexter. They'd reported that, as Dexter himself had said, the journey time would vary depending on the traffic, since there were few opportunities for overtaking. It had taken them fifty minutes to Swindon and another thirty to Beckworth. But suppose Dexter hadn't stopped in Swindon at all? The Buttery had been unable to say if he was there or not, and according to the DCs it hadn't seemed the kind of place which would welcome leisurely diners.

His mind circling round new possibilities, Webb signalled to Jackson and they took their leave of the Parrishes.

"Don't tell me, Guv," Jackson said resignedly as he closed the gate. "We're off to London tomorrow, right?"

"Right, Ken. Friend Dexter has some more explaining to do."

It was a pleasant, leafy suburb in which they found themselves the next morning, with church bells ringing over the sunlit peace. The woman who opened the door was pale and red-eyed, and she bit her lip on seeing Webb's warrant card.

"Mr. Dexter's waiting for you," she said quietly, stepping aside for them to enter.

"Mrs. Kingdom?"

"That's right."

"I understand you're old friends of the Dexters?"

"Yes. They lived just down the road until a few months ago."

"Had you been in touch with Mrs. Dexter recently?"

"She phoned last week."

"And how did she seem?"

"Nervous, edgy, unhappy."

"Why, did she say?"

"The place was getting her down. No one ever spoke to her and she was bored out of her mind."

"You said she was nervous. Of what?"

"She didn't expect to be murdered, if that's what you mean." The woman's voice broke. "Sorry," she murmured after a moment. "She mentioned the village boys, that they'd been scribbling on her door and making comments when she passed them. 'Creepy' was the word she used."

Stewart Dexter appeared in an open doorway and, murmuring an excuse, Mrs. Kingdom left them with him.

"Have you caught him?" he greeted them, an edge to his voice.

"Not yet, sir. We've a few more questions, though."

"Come in, then."

"I believe," Webb said, when they'd seated themselves, "that you and your wife had words last weekend?"

Dexter stared at him. "Where the hell did you dig that up?"

"You were overheard, sir."

"I can't think how."

"You quarrelled about Mr. Carey giving her a lift?"

"Not specifically, though that came into it." He sighed and ran a hand through his hair. "As it turned out, it was all a misunderstanding anyway. I'd mislaid my watch which needed repairing. I was sure I'd left it on the tallboy, but I found it later in the glove compartment of the car."

"You thought your wife had moved it?"

"Not exactly." He flushed. "I'm ashamed to say I suspected our milkman of taking it."

"Your *milkman?*"

"He does some gardening for us occasionally. It seems a plug in the bedroom fused while Carol was hoovering, and since he was there, she asked him to change it for her. He was alone in the room for several minutes, and I—well, I thought he might have nicked it."

*She should have known no one here could be trusted.* "Your wife said she was glad of someone to talk to. Who was she referring to?"

"Joe, I suppose."

"And you blamed her for leaving him alone up there?"

Dexter nodded. "That's why I didn't try to persuade her to come with us to Woodstock."

"And you still maintain that you stopped at the Buttery, even though if you'd kept going you'd have been home in half an hour?"

Dexter held his eyes defiantly. "I do."

"When we last met, sir, I asked what your wife was frightened of and you said the village boys."

"That's right."

"But you didn't mention the graffiti on your door."

"Didn't I? Well, it was part and parcel of the same thing."

"But that did specifically upset her?"

"Yes, it seemed to."

"Did she give you the impression she knew who'd done it?"

"We both assumed it was the Bruisers. It was the fact that they'd actually crept up our path that disturbed her."

"When did you discover it?"

"Wednesday last week."

No hesitation there, at least. Webb thought for a moment. "Could you describe the drawing, sir? Better still, could you draw it for us?" He nodded to Jackson, who extracted a piece of paper from his briefcase and handed it over with his pen. After a moment's thought, Dexter drew a crude circular face and embellished it with tight coils of hair, squinting eyes and a protruding tongue. Then he handed it back. Webb studied it in silence. It was exactly as described by both Mrs. Cummings and Neil Carey, yet neither of them had been alarmed by it.

"There were no initials, or anything that might be construed as a personal threat?"

"No, just the face."

"Very well, Mr. Dexter, that's all for the moment." He rose to his feet. "How are your children adapting to their mother's death?"

"They're all right. I was up there yesterday. It's good for them to have their cousins around; helps to take their mind off things."

They were back in Broadshire by mid-afternoon, and drove directly to Beckworth. Perhaps since Mrs. Dexter had been "glad of someone to talk to," she'd confided her fears to Joe Barlow, who helped in her garden and mended her fuses. At least it was worth a try.

Beckworth House was open again, and they caught a glimpse of Bert Barlow at his kiosk as they turned into Tinker's Lane. The car-park was full and blue uniforms moved systematically between the vehicles. It was unlikely that today's drivers would be any more help than yesterday's, but there was always an outside chance.

It was Barlow himself who opened the door to them.

"Good afternoon, sir. Recovered from your upset?"

"I'm a bit better, yes."

"Then if we could have another word—?"

He led the way to the cluttered kitchen.

"Mr. Barlow, you told us you helped Mrs. Dexter in her garden, so presumably you spoke to her from time to time."

"Only chit-chat."

"Did she ever touch on anything personal—about how she was finding village life, for example?"

He shook his head. "Not that I recall."

"She told her husband she was glad of you to talk to."

Barlow looked surprised. "Did she? Well," he went on

after a moment, "she talked, certainly, but only about the house and the improvements they'd made."

"She didn't hint that she was sorry they'd come?"

"Far from it."

"Then she was putting on a brave front," Webb said, "because in fact she was very unhappy." He saw the man's disbelief and continued, "She'd been uprooted from family and friends, she was alone all day with not much to do, and she wouldn't even have her children at home for the holidays. Added to which the local lads were giving her a hard time and had got her thoroughly nervy. I reckon by the day she died she must have been in a pretty bad way."

"But that can't be right!" Joe protested forcefully. "When I went inside to change a fuse for her she took me all over, showing me where they'd knocked down walls, put in windows, Lord knows what. And she was as pleased as Punch with everything. Now you tell me she was unhappy—it just doesn't add up."

"Perhaps she was trying to convince herself they'd done the right thing." Webb paused. "You say you changed a fuse for her. When was that?"

"Tuesday of last week."

Which, as luck would have it, was before the face appeared on her door, so no chance of an angle on her reactions.

"What makes you think she was unhappy?" Barlow demanded, still not accepting it.

"Her husband told us. So did her best friend in London, and so did Mr. Carey."

He shook his head in bewilderment. "I'd never have believed it, never."

Webb shrugged. "We all erect barriers for ourselves, and our tragedy is that no one bothers to look behind them."

Catching Jackson's raised eyebrow, Webb cleared his throat and stood up. Barlow accompanied them to the door in silence.

"He didn't like to think she'd been unhappy, did he?" Jackson commented in the car.

"Hence my attempt at philosophy. He's probably wishing he'd responded more to her chatter. When it's too late, we all blame ourselves for not doing more."

"There you go again! I reckon a cup of tea would do you a power of good, Guv, and me too, come to that."

Webb grinned tiredly. "You could be right, Ken. We'll look in at the mobile canteen."

Half an hour later, fortified by their tea, they crossed the road to Beckworth House and rang the bell at the gate. They waited for several minutes without result, and were about to turn away when they saw Mrs. Carey coming down the drive in jacket and jodhpurs, a riding hat in her hand. Catching sight of them, she quickened her steps and came to open the gate.

"I'm sorry, Chief Inspector. Have you been waiting long?"

"Only a minute or two."

"I've been exercising the Duke's horses," she explained as they followed her up the path. "One of the perks of my job."

"Your husband's not at home?"

"No, he and Pippa have gone to the Garden Centre." They had entered the minute hall and she pushed open the door of the living-room. "How can I help you this time?"

"About that graffiti, Mrs. Carey; I don't want to alarm you, but I think you should be on your guard."

"How do you mean?"

"We've now discovered that five houses in the village were daubed. You know about the Dexters, and of the others two have since been burgled."

"You mean it was a kind of—statement of intent?"

"I very much hope not, but it's a possibility we can't overlook."

"But why warn us, put us on our guard?"

"I've not the slightest idea."

"I thought it was just something the village boys had been up to."

"It may still be, though none of them have admitted it. It might have no connection whatever with what happened afterwards, but until we know for certain we mean to take no chances. So we're checking to see if any of you noticed anything else in the last week or two that struck you as strange or unusual." He saw her brows pucker uncertainly. "However unimportant it might seem," he added encouragingly.

"Well, I can't really see that it's relevant, but there was a car parked fairly late at night."

"Parked where, Mrs. Carey?"

"In the estate car-park, which is beneath my bedroom window. I saw it twice this last week. I thought it might have been one of yours?" Her voice ended on an almost pleading note, but Webb shook his head.

"None of ours was parked there. You hadn't seen it before?"

"No, but that doesn't mean anything. I only noticed it because another car's headlights lit it up."

"What make was it?"

She shrugged helplessly. "I've no idea. I could only see the roof and a distorted view of the bonnet. I can't even tell you the colour, because on both occasions it had gone by the morning."

"Do you remember which nights it was there?"

"Wednesday and Thursday."

"Not Monday?" When Carol Dexter had met her death.

"I didn't see it then."

"And not since Thursday?"

"No, I made a point of looking. I think I heard it drive away on Thursday, just as I was falling asleep, but I couldn't be bothered to get up and look."

"You don't know what time it arrived?"

She shook her head. "I didn't take much notice till the

second time, and it hasn't been back since. I'm more or less certain of that, because I've kept looking at odd times over the last three days."

Webb said curiously, "Why did you attach significance to it? A car parked in a car-park isn't exactly unusual."

"But that particular car-park's part of the estate and used only by visitors to the House. No one from the village would think of parking there. And it was tucked right into the corner, as though it didn't want to be seen." She gave an uncertain laugh. "I'm probably just being fanciful."

"I hope you are, Mrs. Carey," Webb said heavily, "I very much hope you are."

# CHAPTER 10

Webb said, "The first thing I want to do is have a word with the Barlow lad." He looked up at Jackson, who was gazing out of the window. "Ken?"

Jackson gave a start and turned. "Sorry, Guv. What was that?"

Webb leaned back in his chair and surveyed him. "Something on your mind, Ken? I don't think you've heard a word I've said this morning."

"Sorry. We had a bad night with young Paul again."

"What's the matter with him?"

"Could be a grumbling appendix, the doctor said."

"Good Lord! Can't anything be done?"

"They seem to think it will pass off. Anyway, the kids are still on holiday, so Millie'll be able to keep an eye on him." He straightened, putting personal worries behind him. "What were you saying, Guv?"

"That we ought to see young Barlow at the Whistle Stop and get some low-down on the so-called 'Beckworth

Bruisers'. He was home over Easter, too. Might have seen something."

Jackson nodded. "That's the pub the Drug Squad are interested in, isn't it?"

"Yep; I wonder if the Barlows know that. We might as well go straight along, they've opted to be Open All Hours."

As a reminder that it was after all only the first week in April, the mild weather they'd enjoyed over Easter had given way to a heavy overnight frost and this morning, though the sun still shone, there was an icy wind.

The further you drove along Station Road, Jackson thought, pulling down the sun shield, the tattier the surroundings became. The cheap chain stores, betting shops and pawn-brokers, and the crowded little terrace houses that led off it could have been a million miles rather than a few hundred yards from the prosperity of Gloucester Circus and the smart shops in Carlton Road and East Parade.

The Whistle Stop was an old-fashioned building on the corner of the station approach. Its faded sign bore a picture of a railway porter in peaked cap holding a whistle to his mouth. Jackson turned into the station forecourt and, ignoring the belligerent stares of a group of taxi-drivers, propped his log-book against the windscreen. Then, turning up their coat collars, the two men walked back to the pub, heads bent into the wind.

The door to the public bar had flaking blue paint and a dirty yellow glass panel. Webb pushed it open and went in, Jackson at his heels. Their arrival could not have had more effect if they'd been in uniform. Three men seated at one of the tables hurriedly gathered their belongings together and, avoiding eye contact with the newcomers, made their way quickly and silently outside. Webb let them go. Their activities were not his concern and no doubt they would be followed. He glanced round the small, smoke-hazed room. An elderly man in a corner shifted uneasily, took a draught from his glass, and returned to the betting page of his newspaper. Two younger men on barstools, though clearly on edge, held their ground with defiant bravado.

Webb turned to the barman, a greasy-looking individual in a filthy apron. "A man called Barlow works here. Is he about?"

The man relaxed slightly, grateful that on this occasion at least he was not the object of their interest.

"He's on the late shift today, mate."

"So where will he be?"

The man jerked his head towards an open door behind the bar. "Upstairs having a kip, if I know Darren." He grinned ingratiatingly.

"Would you ask him to come down, please?" Webb produced his warrant card, aware that his general identity was already known. The barman hesitated, eyeing the till, and Webb added pointedly, "I'll keep an eye on things till you get back."

He turned, leaning back against the bar and letting his eyes move over the unsavoury surroundings: scuffed unpolished woodwork, tables stained with rings from countless glasses, dusty red curtains at grimy windows. Hardly an inviting place to relax in.

A clatter of returning footsteps made him turn as the barman reappeared. "He'll be right down," he reported, and, moving further along the bar, made a low-voiced comment to the two seated there which produced an appreciative snigger in reply.

Darren Barlow, bleary-eyed and hair uncombed, came sullenly into the bar.

"Gentlemen here want a word with you," the barman called officiously.

Aware of listening ears, Webb said shortly, "We'll go to the station café," and thankfully pushed his way out into the cold but blessedly fresh air. Darren Barlow, shoulders hunched and fists dug into the pockets of his denim jacket, walked beside him. He might have tried drugs, Webb reflected, but he didn't seem to be on them now, which was something. All the same, he had a police record and was unlikely to be cooperative.

The station café was almost deserted at this hour on a Monday morning. The urns hissed in the background, and the hard white strip-light did nothing to enhance the plastic-looking sandwiches. Even Jackson, nearly always hungry, averted his eyes and ordered only coffee, carrying it to the table where Webb and Barlow awaited him near the comforting ridges of a radiator.

"When did you leave home after Easter?" Webb began, gingerly lifting his polystyrene cup.

"Tuesday, wasn't it? End of the holiday."

"Did you go to Beckworth House while you were there?"

Darren made a derisive sound. "You must be joking."

"Does that mean you didn't?"

"No. I mean yes—I didn't go."

"Did you know the woman who was killed?"

The boy darted a glance at him with his mother's eyes, which in his face had a habitual shiftiness. "Might have seen her around."

"You knew her by sight?"

"Can't say. I've seen some of 'em along the top road, but I dunno which one she was."

"She lived at Coppins Farmhouse."

"Yeah. All right for some. We used to live there, and all."

Webb couldn't hide his surprise. "You did?"

"Well, the family, like. Before I was born. Farmed it for generations."

"They owned it?"

"Tenant farmers. It *belonged* to the Duke, like the rest of bloody Beckworth."

"Why did they leave it?"

"Grandad fell off the barn roof, didn't he? Flat on his back for months and never walked again. Dad was only fourteen so there was nothing for it but to get out."

"So they moved to Tinker's Lane?"

"Yeah, thanks to 'is Grace. Big deal."

Webb turned this new information over in his mind. "And another farmer took on Coppins?"

"That's right. George Powell. Him and his sons ran it till a few years back. Then the old man died and his sons moved into agricultural machinery, and the place was empty for a while."

Ripe pickings for developers, Webb thought, and very lucrative for the already bulging coffers of the Hampshire estate.

"In view of that," he commented, after another sip of scalding coffee, "I'm willing to bet you knew damn well who Mrs. Dexter was, if only because she lived in your family home."

Darren flushed. "All right, then, I knew her by sight. Toffee-nosed bint."

"There's no call to be offensive, Barlow. The woman's dead, after all." He paused. "I suppose a lot of your old pals are still in the village?"

Surprised at the change of subject, Darren nodded warily.

"You keep in touch?"

"We have a jar when I'm home."

"And you all resent the newcomers, consider them 'toffee-nosed'?"

"Well, they are. Not proper villagers at all."

"So you annoy them at every opportunity? Make them jump out of the way of your motorbike, for instance?" As Giles Parrish had related.

"No harm in that," Darren said sulkily.

"And go round scribbling on their doors?"

He could have sworn the boy's blank look was genuine. "Do what?"

"Did you or your buddies draw faces on various front doors in the village?"

*"Faces?* Of course we didn't. That's kids' stuff."

"Would you know if any of the others had?"

"Yeah, we compare notes."

"Scoring points for who's been the biggest nuisance?"

Darren's silence was confirmation that he'd hit the mark. "Have you any idea who might be responsible, then?"

He shook his head. "Kids' stuff," he repeated scornfully. "Nothing to do with us."

Webb said thoughtfully, "You could have had a special grudge against Mrs. Dexter, with her living at Coppins."

The boy sat bolt upright, alarm in his eyes. "Oh, now look, you're not hanging that on me. Why should I, anyway? Not as if we had to get out to make room for her—it happened years ago."

Which, Webb had to concede, was no more than the truth. Another interesting sideline had led them precisely nowhere.

"Finished your report, Sal?" Harry Sage bent over her, his hand familiarly on her shoulder.

"Not quite, Skipper."

"How about a break for lunch, then? We still have a rain-cheque on that drink."

"I don't think so, thanks. I usually just go to the canteen."

"Don't worry, I'll pick up the bill. There's a new pizzeria in Fenton Street—we can give it a try."

"I really—"

His hand tightened, kneading her shoulder, and an edge crept into his voice. "Not being very friendly, are we, Constable? Still carrying the torch for your fancy man? You know the best remedy for that, don't you?"

"It's just—"

"No more excuses. Get your handbag and let's go."

As they went together down the stairs, Sally was hoping desperately that the DCI would appear with an urgent task for her. But there was no one about and, despairingly, she walked with head high past the ornamental pond in the forecourt of the police station and out on to the thronged pavement.

Sage took her arm as they crossed Franklyn Road—an unnecessary precaution since there was no traffic in sight—and when she attempted to free herself on the opposite pavement, simply tightened his hold. Short of making a scene, there was nothing she could do. There was a rank, male smell about him, compounded of imperfectly disguised sweat, tobacco and aftershave, and Sally held down a shudder of distaste.

The pizzeria when they reached it was dimly lit and featured discreet little booths, each containing a table with a candle stuck in a Chianti bottle. There was an overpowering smell of garlic. Automatically she took the menu the waiter handed her. At least there were people about, she told herself. This was better by far than a parked car in Chantock Forest. With a bright smile she chose her pizza, hoping she wouldn't choke on it. Perhaps after all he was only being friendly.

A bottle of Chianti arrived but Sally, who never drank at lunch-time, dared make no further demur. She sipped the wine slowly, feeling it rough on her tongue and trying to ignore the pressure of Sage's leg under the table. Friendly, my eye! she thought, and was grateful when the food arrived to distract him.

Throughout the meal she chatted lightly about the Beckworth case, blocking any opportunity for the conversation to turn personal. She was careful to cover her glass each time Sage lifted the bottle, with the result that he topped up his own instead. Even the small amount she had drunk made her head ache and, she realized in dismay, Sage's much larger intake was also having an effect. He was now leaning permanently towards her, his hand frequently brushing against hers, and beneath the table the pressure of his knee had increased. The sooner they got back to the station, Sally thought fervently, the better.

The meal over at last, she stood up thankfully and bent to retrieve her handbag. But in the same moment Sage rounded the table, and as she straightened she felt his hand on her buttocks. She turned swiftly to find him close against her, and before she could evade him his hot, searching mouth closed over hers. Foolish to have felt safe, when the wooden cubicles offered such unwelcome privacy. Which, no doubt, was why he'd chosen the place. Though she was struggling fiercely to free herself, it was the approaching steps of the waiter that rescued her.

"Atta girl, Sal," Sage said thickly. "You scratch my back and I'll scratch yours. In a manner of speaking."

Back at the police station Sally made straight for the cloakroom, where she scrubbed furiously at her mouth with soap and water. Then, gathering her shredded dignity about her, she went to see Inspector Petrie.

Since burglary and murder had disrupted the first week of their holiday, the Cummingses were determined to get maximum value from the second. Each day's activities had been exhaustively discussed and planned, and that Monday they'd elected to go to Bristol and look over the great iron ship that was moored there.

However, as they were finishing breakfast Edith Irving made a theatrical appearance in her dressing-gown, announcing that she'd hardly closed her eyes all night, that she had shooting pains in her head, and that Gina must take her to the doctor without delay. Nothing that any of them said could dissuade her, and she was therefore driven, hand clasped to her forehead, to the nearest doctor, who happened to be in Lethbridge. There, after a long wait at the surgery, she was given a prescription for something resembling aspirin and told to rest quietly, which, as Bob did not hesitate to point out, had been the remedy he'd suggested in the first place.

There was another long wait at the chemist while the prescription was made up, resulting in a totally wasted morning and a late lunch, by which time tempers were frayed all round.

With the aim of retrieving something from the shambles, Bob suggested to his sons that they take the dog for a walk in the woods. Gina, it was accepted, would be unable to accompany them, since her mother refused to be left alone "in her state of health."

"What an old misery-guts Gran is!" Duncan commented as they set off at last. "I don't know how Mum puts up with her!"

"Oh, she's not a bad old stick," Andrew replied. "She likes to be the centre of attention, that's all, and since we came here she hasn't been."

Which, Bob reflected silently, summed up his mother-in-law pretty astutely.

It was a perfect day for a walk, and an agreeable sense of male comradeship soon dispelled their frustrations. They entered the forest at its uppermost limit, striking out along the well-trodden paths while the spaniel, in a frenzy of delight, set off in search of imaginary rabbits and squirrels, and had to be called back at frequent intervals in case he got lost. Despite the well-marked tracks, they had vast expanses of woodland to themselves, for the forest, popular with weekend visitors, retreated into its silences during the week. Only down by the camping site was there much sign of life, and the Cummingses gave that a wide berth.

Time passed as they threw sticks for the dog, discussed the weekend's rugby matches and examined the different kinds of leaves beginning to appear. Bob, forgetting they'd started out late, was surprised when the light beneath the trees began to dim, and, glancing at his watch, discovered it was after six. It was also getting colder, he realized as soon as he stopped walking.

"Hey, we must be getting back," he exclaimed. "Your mother will be wondering where we are. Come to think of it, I'm not so sure myself!"

He paused, surveying the lie of the land. They'd been

walking aimlessly, first in one direction, then another, and had covered a fair bit of ground. To his relief the distant sound of a car reached them, and they turned in the direction from which it had come.

"Where's Kip?" Bob asked after a few minutes, looking about him.

"He ran ahead."

"Well, it's time he went back on his lead; we don't want him disappearing at this stage. From the look of it, it'll be dark soon."

Andrew put his fingers to his mouth and gave the piercing whistle which usually brought the dog running. This time, however, though they also called his name, there was no sign of him.

"I hope he's not stuck in a rabbit hole," Duncan said anxiously.

"He's probably shot off on some trail or other. If we keep calling he's sure to hear us."

"*Kip!*" yelled Duncan again, and this time, some distance away, an excited yapping sounded in reply. "Here, boy! Good dog!"

They stood waiting expectantly but, though the barking continued spasmodically, the dog still didn't appear. Bob said irritably, "What's the matter with the animal? His only good point is that he comes when he's called."

"It's a funny kind of bark," Andrew said uneasily. "I think we'd better go and look for him."

The occasional shrill yaps were coming from ahead and slightly to the left of the path they were following. Swearing under his breath, Bob turned off into the undergrowth and the boys overtook him, calling the dog's name. Beneath his irritation, he was aware of disquiet. Kip *was* obedient, but even now, when they must be quite close to him, he was not responding to their calls. Could he be caught in a trap?

Then Andrew's relieved voice reached him. "There he

is! Come on, boy!" And then, with a change of tone, "What is it? What have you found?"

Bob stopped, waiting for them to come back and join him. Somewhere in the branches overhead there was a rustle of wings and a harsh cry. Despite himself he shivered. And suddenly Andrew reappeared, his face white in the shadows. Bob had just time to think, "Oh God, it *is* a trap!" before the boy said in a quavering voice, "Dad, it's Mr. Carey from the Lodge. His throat's been cut."

"But you must be mistaken," Alison repeated patiently. "He can't be dead—his dinner's in the oven."

All in all, Sally thought, this was proving to be quite a day. At least, after her talk with Inspector Petrie, she had Liz Denton with her instead of the odious Sage. She took Alison's arm and led her into the tiny living-room.

"Perhaps we could have a cup of tea?" she suggested, submerging her helpless pity in routine.

"I don't want tea," Mrs. Carey said, her voice rising. "We'll be having dinner as soon as my husband gets home." She glanced at the clock. "Which should be any minute now."

The sound of the front door reached them and she added triumphantly, "There! What did I tell you?"

Sally turned sharply, a primeval shiver moving coldly down her spine, but it was a flesh-and-blood girl who stood in the doorway. Before she could speak, Mrs. Carey said clearly, "Darling, these people are trying to say something's happened to Daddy."

The girl's eyes flew to Sally. "What is it? What's happened?"

Sally's fingernails dug into her palms. She'd never get used to this. "I'm very sorry, Miss Carey, but—"

"He's dead?"

Sally nodded, and the girl hurled herself across the room into her mother's arms, which rose hesitantly to receive her. Above her bent head and shaking body, Mrs. Carey's eyes met Sally's, the first doubt in them.

"Neil's dead?"

"Yes. I'm so sorry."

The girl started to sob quietly but the woman remained calm. In shock, Sally thought.

"A car crash?"

"No, I'm afraid his death was deliberate."

The girl turned at that, her tear-stained face paling. "You mean he was murdered? Like Mrs. Dexter?"

"It's possible." Suicide hadn't been ruled out, but would that be any comfort? She added, "He'd have died very quickly."

Mrs. Carey moistened her lips. "Where is he? I must go to him."

The girl shuddered a protest but Sally was already shaking her head. "Not just yet. There are—doctors with him at the moment."

"Where did it happen?" Though still dry-eyed, she'd started to shake and a tremor had come into her voice.

"In the forest below the village."

"The *forest?* But what was he doing there?"

Sally raised her shoulders helplessly. "That's what we'll have to find out."

Putting her daughter gently aside, Alison Carey felt behind her for a chair and lowered herself carefully into it. Then she looked up at the sombre policewomen. "I think perhaps we should have that tea after all," she said.

"And when we came to the road, by one of those lay-by places, we saw his car."

Bob Cummings was sitting with a glass of whisky at his side, opposite a grim-faced Webb. Gina hovered solicitously at his side and the two boys, unnaturally subdued, were on the sofa. Of the old woman, thankfully, there was as yet no sign. Having upbraided them over her daughter's finding one body, Webb shuddered to think of her reaction to her grandsons discovering another.

"Were any other cars there?"

"No."

"Not even your own?"

"No; we'd walked down, but through the woods. We hadn't been near the road until then."

"And this was at six-fifteen, you said."

"Give or take a couple of minutes."

Webb was silent for a while, reviewing such facts as he had. He'd stopped at the scene on the way up: the murdered man's car had been tidily parked, and his body lay some hundred yards into the forest. Either he'd stopped voluntarily and for some reason walked into the woods, or he'd been flagged down and led to his death. There seemed no logic in either hypothesis, certainly not robbery, since his watch and full wallet were on his body.

Bob Cummings cleared his throat. "Do you think there's a connection between the two deaths, Chief Inspector?"

"It's too early to say, sir." Carey and Mrs. Dexter had known each other, but only briefly. The other link they had was shared by the Cummingses among others—the graffiti on their doors. The appalling possibility of three more deaths to come was not one to dwell on.

"You're no nearer finding who killed Mrs. Dexter?" Mrs. Cummings was asking.

"There are various leads," Webb said enigmatically, avoiding Jackson's eye.

"I feel so sorry for her husband. Poor man, he was looking very drawn today."

Webb sat forward so suddenly that she jumped. "Mr. Dexter was here today?"

She stared at him with rounded eyes. "Yes, this afternoon. He'd come to collect some things."

"What time was this, Mrs. Cummings?"

"About half past five, I suppose."

"When he arrived, or when he left?"

"When he left. I watched him drive away."

"I see." And he did see. If Stewart Dexter had left home about five-thirty, he might well have encountered Neil Carey on the road through the woods.

# CHAPTER 11

*"Now,* Guv?"

"Yes, now, Ken. We don't want to lose any time on this."

"But—we don't even know he'll be there. Shouldn't we phone first?"

"And tip him off? Not on your nelly. I know it's late to be setting off for London, but in the circumstances it can't be helped."

Jackson sighed and started the car. All day the worry about Paul had been at the back of his mind, and he'd been glad when it was time to go home. But as he was on the point of leaving the news about Neil Carey came through. Now, with a trip to London ahead of them, it would be well past midnight before he got home. He'd have liked to phone Millie but there was no sign of a public call-box, and the determined set of the Governor's jaw suggested any delay would be unwelcome.

"We'll see just how long it takes to get there," Webb was adding. "Friend Dexter's travelling times are eccentric, as we know. It's now eight-fifteen: unless he stopped off in Chantock Forest, he should be arriving just about now."

"Mrs. Cummings only said *about* five-thirty," Jackson pointed out, "and he could have been caught in the rush-hour."

"Carey was found at six-fifteen and judging by body temperature had been dead only minutes. Which means if

Dexter's our man, he wouldn't have got away before six at the earliest. Provided he arrived in London before eight-thirty, he's in the clear. If not—" Webb lifted his shoulders.

"You're thinking he might have killed his missus and then come back to do for her feller?"

"There's no evidence Carey *was* her feller, though given time he might have been." Webb made a dismissive gesture. "No, my thoughts are nothing like as definite as that. I just want to see Dexter as soon as possible and gauge his mood. If he *has* just topped Carey, there might be something to show for it."

They were approaching the M4, a roaring channel of rushing headlights. Jackson eased the car down the slope and cautiously joined the continuous stream, to be immediately swallowed up in its frenetic anonymity.

By the light of the street-lamp, they checked that it was just on eleven as they knocked on the door of the Kingdoms' house. A light still showed in the hall, though both bedroom windows were also lit. Nice thing it would be, Jackson thought, if after all this no one came to let them in.

Catching an echo of his thought, Webb knocked again. It was cold, a frost sheening the grass of the lawn to their right. "Come *on!*" he muttered under his breath, rubbing his hands together. In response the bulb in the porch flowered suddenly into light and, with the sound of sliding bolts, the front door opened at last and Raymond Kingdom stood peering out at them.

"Who is it? What do you want at this time of night?" He sounded irritated but not alarmed, proof that, despite the much-trumpeted increase in crime, the citizens of leafy England still did not fear the late-night knock at the door.

"Shillingham police, Mr. Kingdom. Sorry to disturb you so late, but we'd like a word with Mr. Dexter."

"Good grief!" Kingdom grumbled. "Surely it could have waited till morning? The poor chap's gone to bed." But he stepped aside and gestured for them to enter.

"Could you tell me, sir," Webb said casually, relishing the welcoming warmth of the house, "what time he got back this evening?"

"Later than usual, because he'd been to Beckworth. We held dinner back for him."

"Could you put a time on it, sir?" Webb persisted.

"Oh, between eight and half past. Why?" he added, suddenly suspicious.

Webb ignored the question. "You're certain of that? It could be important."

"Well, you'd better ask him yourself." He turned, called up the stairs, "Stewart! Some chaps here to see you!" and opened the door of the room they'd been in previously. The television muttered quietly in a corner, the newspaper lay discarded on the floor, and the cushions on the vacated chairs were comfortably dented. It looked like hundreds of other late-evening rooms all over the country and Jackson felt a stab of longing for his own, and the sound of Millie's knitting needles and Paul safely asleep upstairs. And at the thought of his son, the worm of worry began to gnaw again.

Stewart Dexter appeared in the doorway in pyjamas and dressing-gown. "Chief Inspector? You've found out who killed my wife?"

"Drawn" was the word Gina Cummings had used to describe him, and it was an apt one. His eyes were haunted and sunken, but whether from loss or guilt, Webb could not be certain. "Not yet, sir."

The man's face fell. "I was sure, when you came so late, it must be that."

"Could you tell me, Mr. Dexter, what time you got back here this evening?"

His expression was purely surprise, Jackson would have bet on it. "Tonight? Not till after eight. Why?"

"Can you be more exact, sir?"

"Probably, but can you give me any reason why I

should?" Hope and disappointment had, in the face of questioning, given way to resentment.

"Where were you this afternoon?"

"I went to Beckworth. I'm surprised your spies didn't tell you."

"Why was that?"

"Why did I go to my own house? I'm damned if I see that it's any of your business."

"Mr. Dexter, you're entitled to an explanation, and you'll get it in a moment. In the meantime, I'd be grateful if you'd answer my questions. Exactly what time did you get back here?"

"Just before eight-fifteen. I sat in the car at the gate to catch the end of the programme I'd been listening to."

Which time, roughly confirmed by Kingdom, was within the leeway Webb had allowed.

"And your reasons for visiting Beckworth?"

Dexter's jaw tightened, but he answered steadily. "To collect some papers I needed."

"When you drove down to the main road, did you notice any cars parked in the lay-bys in the wood?"

"Not that I remember. Why?"

"Did any cars pass you, going up the hill?"

"One or two."

"Any you recognized?"

"I only glanced at them."

"And you didn't stop for any reason as you drove through the wood?"

"No, I did not. Look, what is this? Are you telling me you got me out of bed at this time of night to answer damn-fool questions about lay-bys?"

Webb sighed, abandoning his most promising suspect. "Mr. Neil Carey died in the woods this evening."

Dexter stared at him. *'Died?* What the hell do you mean, died?"

"Was probably murdered," Webb said.

"My God!" Dexter sat down suddenly on the arm of a

chair. Then indignation struggled through shock. "And you thought I'd something to do with it?"

"Mr. Dexter, these are routine inquiries. We're trying to find your wife's killer, and now Mr. Carey's. Surely you want that?"

"Not," said Dexter, with a touch of wry humour, "if you've selected me for the part."

"They'd been together that afternoon in Lethbridge."

"That's a motive for murder?"

"It could be."

Dexter made a sound of disbelief. "But you did know I'd been back there. How? Ah—Mrs. Cummings. I saw her as I was leaving."

"It came out quite innocently. She was concerned about you."

"Nice of her. And on the strength of that you come haring over here after me? You must be pretty desperate."

Yes, Webb thought tiredly, we are.

"How was he killed? Not drowned, like Carol?"

"No, his throat was cut. There's an outside chance it was suicide, but he'd a bruise not consistent with the way he fell."

"So there's a homicidal maniac loose up there. Thank God I moved the kids out when I did."

There was a tap on the door, and Mrs. Kingdom came in, also wearing a dressing-gown. Her eyes went to Dexter, full of concern. "Are you all right, Stewart?"

"Yes, I'm all right. They came over on a wild-goose chase."

She closed her eyes with a sigh of relief, then turned to Webb. "You're going back to Broadshire tonight?"

"Yes, ma'am, we'll be on our way. Sorry for disturbing you."

"Have you had anything to eat?"

Webb hesitated, catching Jackson's eye. "No, there hasn't been time. We've another murder on our hands, I'm afraid. Mr. Neil Carey." He paused, watching her to see if the name meant anything, if perhaps either of the Dexters had mentioned him, but her shocked exclamation was quite impersonal.

"How dreadful—I am sorry. But you've a long drive ahead of you; would you like some coffee and sandwiches?"

"That's extremely kind of you."

It was a quarter to midnight when they left the Kingdoms' house, but the food and hot drink had put new life in them. Now they were homeward bound, Jackson's spirits rose. No doubt he'd been worrying unnecessarily and Millie'd tell him Paul was over the upset. Children were up and down so quickly.

His optimism lasted until, home at last, he put his key in the front door. But as he pushed it open something about the quality of the stillness resurrected his fears, even before his eyes fell on the note on the hall table. He caught it up with a rush of fear, holding it to the light so his tired eyes could make out Millie's scrawl.

*8.0 p.m. Have gone to the General with Paul. Children with Mary. Please come as soon as you can.*

Eight P.M.! It was now after two in the morning and she hadn't come back! To make sure, he went up the stairs two at a time, looking in one empty bedroom after another. Two minutes later he was back in the car and driving swiftly through the deserted night streets, past the entrance to the police station to the general hospital next door.

"Paul Jackson!" he repeated urgently to the nurse on the desk. "My son. Probably an appendicitis. He came in about eight."

"Oh yes, the little boy. Just one moment." She spoke briefly into a phone while Jackson tried to hold down his fear. He'd always hated hospitals, and in the middle of the night their unnatural brilliance and bustle struck cold terror into him.

"Churchill Ward," the nurse was saying, "on the first floor. The lifts are over there."

"Is he all right?" Jackson demanded urgently.

"He's out of theatre and back in the ward. Your wife's with him."

No lift had ever moved more slowly. Emerging at last, he stood looking frantically about him, his eyes alighting on the words "Churchill Ward" over the entrance to a large, dimly lit space. Then he was hurrying down the length of it to the closed curtains at the end and fearfully drawing them aside. Millie rose swiftly from the chair beside the bed.

"Ken! Oh thank God! He's going to be all right!" And as his arms closed fumblingly about her, she burst into a torrent of tears.

Banks Moorhouse, a well-known electronics firm, occupied two floors of a building in the centre of Reading. Having spent the night at the hospital, Jackson had taken a day's leave and Webb was accompanied by DC Marshbanks, as eager as a puppy to sniff out suspects.

"He could have learned something to his advantage and been blackmailing someone," he suggested as, following the directions given by the girl on reception, he drove into the private car-park at the rear of the building.

"Indeed he could, Simon," Webb agreed, regretting his own lost enthusiasm, and feeling, as he usually did in Marshbanks's presence, older than his years.

"After all, he was personnel director, wasn't he? He'd have access to private files and so on."

"You reckon his death had nothing to do with Carol Dexter, then?"

"Oh." Briefly abashed, Marshbanks reconsidered swiftly. "Well, perhaps she told him something about her husband, and Carey was blackmailing him."

"Unfortunately," Webb observed, "Mr. Dexter appears to be in the clear. Anyway, let's keep an open mind, shall we, and see what we can learn here."

The staff at Banks Moorhouse had not yet heard of Carey's death, and Webb studied their reactions as he broke the news. Everyone seemed genuinely shocked, and there was nothing to give pause to even the most suspicious mind.

"How long was he with you?" he asked one of the directors.

"About a year, I suppose. Seemed a pleasant, competent chap. Only yesterday he was telling me of some new scheme he'd thought up to facilitate—but you don't want to hear about that."

"Did he ever mention meeting anyone outside the firm?"

"No; being in personnel he'd not much contact with outsiders during working hours. But his secretary's the person to ask about that."

Lucy Fielding was crying quietly over her word-processor when they were shown into her office. An attractive girl in her mid-twenties, she blew her nose as they sat down and tried to compose herself.

"I'm sorry, it's the shock," she said. "I can't really take it in."

"That's all right, miss. Now, can you tell us if Mr. Carey received any phone calls yesterday?"

"Only internal ones."

"Were they private?"

"No, as it happened I was in the room with him each time."

"Did he ever have calls from outside?"

She thought for a minute, then shook her head. "His wife rang once, but I don't remember any others."

"How did he spend his lunch-hours, do you know?"

"He usually went to the wine bar with Mr. Phillips."

Webb made a note to see Mr. Phillips. "Was there anything unusual in his diary, any meetings you hadn't arranged yourself?"

"No, nothing."

"And how did he seem yesterday?"

"The same as always. He brought me a bunch of violets back from lunch." Her eyes brimmed at the memory, going to the delicate flowers in a jar on her desk.

"He often gave you flowers?"

"Sometimes." She added quickly, "It didn't mean anything, it was just his way. 'Here you are, Lucy,' he said, 'here's a breath of spring to cheer your Monday.' " And she reached for her handkerchief again.

Webb waited patiently while she dabbed at her eyes. "Did he ever speak of personal matters? Things that happened at home, for instance?"

"He told me about that woman's murder, and that he'd given her a lift only a couple of days before."

And he himself died one week later. *Could* he have killed Carol? He'd admitted being home at the time. But even if he had, there seemed no way Dexter could have killed *him*, which would have been the tidy solution.

"What time did Mr. Carey leave here last night?"

"A little earlier than usual. He had a dental appointment in the afternoon, and told me he'd be going straight home afterwards."

"You can't put a time on it?"

"Actually, I can. This window overlooks the car-park, and I happened to glance out about four-thirty and saw him getting into his car."

Which explained why he'd reached Chantock Forest around six.

Their meeting with Mr. Phillips was of little help. Yes, he'd usually lunched with Carey, and was clearly shaken by his death. But theirs had been a business comradeship, with no confidences exchanged.

"He did say he was trying to talk his wife into moving closer to Reading," he added. "I gather she wasn't keen." Which was the closest they'd come to discussing personal matters.

With nothing to add to their knowledge of Neil Carey

and his circumstances, Webb and Marshbanks returned to Shillingham.

"Mrs. Carey spoke of seeing a parked car late at night," Webb told a meeting of his men that afternoon. "I want to know if anyone else saw it, particularly any of the clients of the Green Man, which is just across the road. Get on to that, will you. And arrange round-the-clock protection for the old couple in the bungalow. It might be coincidence, but they're the only recipients of graffiti to whom nothing further has happened. I intend to keep it that way."

As they dispersed, Webb sat tapping his pen on his blotter, deep in thought. He was remembering his question to Simon that morning: *You reckon his death had nothing to do with Carol Dexter's?* And the boy's hasty readjustment. But suppose that unspoken assumption had been correct? Suppose it was only by chance that, for completely different reasons, they'd met their deaths within so short a time of each other?

Marshbanks was hovering hopefully just inside the door, like a puppy begging for a walk. Sergeant Jackson would be back tomorrow, after which he'd be relegated to routine work. He intended to make the most of today.

"Anywhere I can drive you, Guv?" he inquired.

Webb pushed back his chair. "Yes, we won't do much good here. Back to Beckworth, then, Simon. The car knows its own way by now."

Hazel Barlow had spent a fair bit of time with Mrs. Carey, he was thinking, and had seen her husband with Carol Dexter. Perhaps that wasn't all she'd seen. Worth sounding her out, anyway.

But at Tinker's Lane their knock was answered by a young, plain woman, heavily pregnant. "Mum's not in," she informed them. "She's up at the greenhouses."

Webb hesitated. "You'll be Mrs.—?"

"Hobbs," the girl supplied.

He nodded, seeing a slight family resemblance to the

obnoxious Darren. "I believe you were up at the House on Easter Monday?"

"I helped out with the teas, yes."

"Did you see Mrs. Dexter, by any chance?"

"No, but I only stayed an hour. I've not to be on my feet too much."

"Did you see anyone you knew up there?"

"Only Grandad on the gate. I've been through all this already," she added, but without rancour. She seemed, in fact, to enjoy being questioned, revelling in the vicarious excitement.

"Did you know Mr. Carey at all?"

The girl gave an exaggerated shiver. "I used to see him round the village before he got a job, like. They're saying *he* was murdered, and all."

"You hadn't seen him lately?"

Regretfully she shook her head.

"Well, thank you for your help." And with Marshbanks at his side, he started back up the road.

Blue uniforms were again in evidence as inquiries got underway on the second murder. And this time last week, the first hadn't been discovered. What smouldering violence had suddenly flared in this formerly peaceful village, extinguishing not one life but two?

To Webb's relief it was WDC Denton, not Mrs. Carey, who came to open the gate for them. He hadn't wanted to express his condolences through the wrought-iron, nor, in fact, to become involved with her at all today. Which was why he'd arranged for Nina Petrie to interview her.

Averting his eyes from the windows of the Lodge, he set off up the drive with Marshbanks at his heels. Discreet signposts pointed the way to the statuary, the maze, the folly. Ignoring them, Webb strode on to the top of the drive, where, circling the House and the walled garden, they at last came to the greenhouses. An elderly man in a frayed cardigan and stained flannels was just emerging from them, a large bunch of freesias in his hand. Webb eyed him suspiciously.

"Is Mrs. Barlow in there?"

"Yes. Yes, she is." His mouth twitched. "I assure you I have her permission to take these."

Webb grunted. No point in telling the old codger it wasn't up to her to give permission. Anyway, he'd more important things on his mind. He pushed open the door and the warm, damp atmosphere flowed over him. Mrs. Barlow was doing her afternoon watering, but she set down the hose and came towards them, rubbing her hands down the sides of her trousers. There was no need to ask if she'd heard of Carey's death.

"I haven't been to the Lodge," she greeted them. "I didn't want to intrude. We just couldn't believe it, Joe and me. Stunned, we were. It just doesn't seem possible."

"Mrs. Barlow, did you ever see Mr. Carey with anyone other than Mrs. Dexter? A man, for instance?"

She stared at him uncomprehendingly. "How do you mean?"

"We're wondering if he had a connection with someone that no one knew about."

"Someone who could have killed him?" she asked, round-eyed.

"That's it."

He waited hopefully for a minute or two, then she shook her head. "He knew everyone in the village, of course, but they don't count."

"Why not?"

She looked surprised. "Well, no one here would have killed him, would they?"

"Or Mrs. Dexter?"

"Of course not." She stopped, a soil-encrusted hand going to her throat. "You're not trying to say it *was* someone from the village? Someone we all know?"

"I'm saying it might have been. But the only known connection between Mrs. Dexter and Mr. Carey, apart from the graffiti and the fact they've both been killed, is the afternoon they went to Lethbridge and you saw them in the car." He paused. "Unless you'd seen them together another time?" Wordlessly she shook her head, her eyes still fixed on his. "Or anyone else with either of them, someone you mightn't have expected?" Another shake.

Webb wiped his hand across his face and unbuttoned his mac. The heat in here was stifling. "I gather from your son that your family used to live at Coppins?"

"You went to see Darren?" She paled, her face glistening under its film of moisture. "Why?"

"Mrs. Barlow," he said patiently, "in a murder investigation, we go to see everyone."

"Oh. Yes, I see."

"About Coppins—"

But she wasn't interested in Coppins. "That was years ago," she said dismissively. "Even before Joe and I started courting."

Webb returned perforce to the matter in hand. "Did Mrs. Carey ever speak about her husband? Mention his friends, and so on?"

"No."

It was not being a profitable interview, and the sudden heat had brought home to Webb how tired he was. Four hours' sleep last night had not done much for him. Turning to go, his eyes fell on a bunch of freesias lying on the side.

"Nice of you to let that old chap have some," he commented.

"Old—?" Hazel giggled, looking suddenly years younger. "That 'old chap'," she said, "happened to be His Grace the Duke of Hampshire."

# CHAPTER 12

Webb recounted his cavalier treatment of the Duke to Hannah that evening. "So if you hear I've been thrown into the Tower, you'll know why!" he ended, stretching out his feet to the fire.

" 'Off with his head!' and all that." She replenished his drink. "I'm sorry you've been landed with a second murder. I caught the news headlines when I got in."

"Yep. And the devil of it is I can't decide if we're after one killer or two."

"In a place the size of Beckworth?"

"Perhaps it's infectious. Both victims had head injuries inflicted before death, though in the woman's case it could have been accidental—caused by a fall, for instance. But the blow didn't kill either of them: one died by drowning, the other from a slit throat."

Hannah shuddered. "I don't envy you your job."

"There are times when I don't envy myself," Webb rejoined, sipping his whisky. "Forgive me if I fall asleep at some point; I didn't get to bed till three this morning."

"Did this second victim know the first?"

"Yes, but as far as I can judge not well. He gave her a lift in his car on Easter Saturday."

"Easter Saturday," Hannah repeated reflectively. "That was the day I was in Beckworth. I never thought it would become the scene of two murders. Who's been killed this time? I didn't catch the name."

"A man called Neil Carey."

"Neil . . ." Hannah creased her brow. "Where did I . . . ?" Then her eyes widened. "David! He didn't live at the Lodge, did he?"

Webb stared at her. "Yes, he did. His wife's booking

manager for Beckworth House. Hannah, what is it? Did
you know him?"

"No, but I overheard a conversation—at the reception.
Gwen and I were round the corner in the ladies' room, and
they didn't realize we were there."

"Who didn't?"

"Mrs.—Carey, did you say? It must have been her—and
one of the guests. I don't know who she was."

"Go on."

"Well, Mrs. Carey must have come into the room, and
this woman knew her. She said she hadn't seen her at the
church, and Mrs. Carey said she wasn't a guest, she worked
there and lived at the Lodge. But then—it was rather awful
really—the woman asked about 'Neil'—did she ever hear of
him."

"*Hear* of him?"

"Yes. And when Mrs. Carey said he was working in
personnel, she made some snide comment about probably
being up to his old tricks."

Webb straightened slowly in his chair.

"You see," Hannah continued, the words falling over
themselves in her excitement, "she thought that after 'the
scandal,' as she called it, they had divorced. But from the
tone of her voice, Mrs. Carey knew nothing about it."

"Ye gods!"

"So then of course the woman hastily back-tracked,
apologized for being tactless and beat a hasty retreat. And a
moment later we heard Mrs. Carey go out, too. Thank
goodness neither realized we were there."

Webb whistled softly. "Think carefully, love. Can you
remember any details the woman let slip before she realized
her faux pas?"

"I don't think there was anything else, just 'up to his
old tricks'. Which could have been anything, I suppose,
from chasing someone round the filing cabinets to blackmail."

"What was that about scandal?"

Hannah frowned, thinking back. "Only that after the scandal and his sudden dismissal she'd assumed they'd separated."

"It must have been pretty serious, then."

"Yes." Hannah sat down slowly opposite him. "David, could Mrs. Carey have killed the Dexter woman? If she found out she'd been with her husband?"

"An interesting suggestion, but she was at a point-to-point with her daughter on Easter Monday. I had her husband on the suspect list, though, and depending on what his 'tricks' were, I could still be right. The fact that he's been killed himself doesn't mean he didn't top Carol Dexter."

"Then"—Hannah's voice shook a little—"if his wife found out what his 'old tricks' were, could she have killed *him?*"

Webb said slowly, "I suppose it's possible. Sally Pierce said she was in shock when she heard of his death. But if she'd killed him herself she would have been, wouldn't she? We'll certainly check her again. The thing is, though, while I accept she might have stuck a knife into him on the spur of the moment, that murder was premeditated. Someone took a knife to the woods with the express purpose of killing Neil Carey, and somehow I don't think that person was his wife. I grant we could all be murderers under sufficient provocation, but I doubt if all of us could plan it in advance."

"Good," Hannah said quietly. The ginger cat came into the room, tail sticking up like a stalk, and, taking permission for granted, leapt lightly on to her knee. Her fingers caressed it absent-mindedly. "Have you seen her since his death?"

"No, I left her to female ministrations, first Sally, then Nina. But according to their statements, she never mentioned his dismissal. She told me herself he'd been out of work when they first went to Beckworth, then he got a job in Reading." He sighed. "It seems hard to drag all this up now, but there's no option. What happened three years ago, or whatever, might be very relevant indeed to what happened yesterday."

When Webb and Jackson were shown into the small living-room at the Lodge the next morning, there was a tall young man standing by the window. Alison Carey, calm and controlled, introduced him as her son Jonathan. It took only a few seemingly innocuous questions to elicit the fact that he had undeniably been at his agricultural college in Wiltshire on Monday evening.

The daughter Philippa was also present, lounging listlessly on the sofa. Webb cleared his throat.

"Mrs. Carey, I'm sorry to trouble you with more questions, but I'm afraid there are still several to be answered. And I think it would be better if we could ask them privately."

The two young people looked up—indignantly? protectively?—but when their mother nodded towards the door, they left the room without protest.

Webb turned from watching them to see her looking steadily at him. "Well, Chief Inspector? What is it that my children can't hear?"

"I'm sorry to have to bring this up, but it could be important. I understand your husband was dismissed from his last job?"

Whatever she'd been expecting, it was not that. Colour flooded her face, then receded, leaving her very pale. "Daphne Warrender?" she asked after a moment.

"I beg your pardon?"

"Was that where you got the information?"

"Possibly, indirectly. You were overheard talking at the Harwood reception."

She raised her eyebrows. "I find that hard to believe. We were alone at the time."

"Some people were round the corner of the cloakroom. The eavesdropping was unintentional."

"But useful," Alison said bitterly.

"If it traces who killed your husband."

That startled her. "You think it might?"

"My informant had the impression you hadn't known of the so-called scandal."

"No," she admitted quietly.

"No doubt you asked your husband that evening for an explanation?"

There was a long pause. Then, without looking at him, she said again, "No."

Webb stared at her. "Mrs. Carey, let me get this straight. Are you telling me that you discovered your husband had been involved in some scandal which resulted in his dismissal, and you didn't tax him with it?"

She raised her head then, her hazel eyes meeting his defiantly. "That's certainly what I'm telling you, Chief Inspector. Whether you believe it or not is up to you."

"But why did you keep silent?"

She spread her hands in a helpless little gesture. "It didn't seem worth all the hassle. I guessed it was to do with women; Neil always had a weakness for them. There'd been rows before, plenty of them, and I just couldn't face another. In any case, it's ancient history now."

"But didn't it alter your feelings for him?"

She gave a twisted smile. "Not to the extent of killing him. Actually," she went on, "I thought long and hard about it all, and I realized that without being aware of it, I'd stopped loving him. He wanted us to move, you know; nearer to Reading and his job. We'd discussed it a few days earlier, but I didn't want to go. So I decided to leave things as they were unless he tried to put pressure on me. If he did, I'd suggest we separated and I stayed where I was. And I'd a good enough reason to give for my decision."

"What did he tell you, when he was suddenly out of a job?" Webb asked curiously.

"That he'd been made redundant. That was what hurt

most last week, remembering how I'd done all I could to keep his spirits up and support him."

"It was then you came here?"

She nodded. "With Neil out of work, our rather hefty mortgage was an increasing burden. So when I was offered this job and the house to go with it, we sold up and put the money in the bank."

"And you still don't know why he really left?"

"No, but I'm sure Daphne does."

"Who exactly is she?"

"The wife of the managing director of Stanley Marcus. We used to go to dinner at each other's houses but it was only business entertaining; I never cared for them. He was pompous and stuffy and she was, well—bitchy, to be honest. I don't doubt she had a field day when she got home from the wedding, ringing up all her friends and telling them that fool Alison was still with Neil."

Webb glanced at Jackson, writing industriously in his pocket-book. "Could we have her name and address, then?"

They lived in Buckinghamshire, which at least, Webb thought thankfully, was reasonably accessible. He took his leave of Mrs. Carey, but not before ascertaining that on Monday afternoon she had been showing prospective clients over the House. It was conceivable that she could have reached the woods in time to kill her husband, but it would have been a close thing. Personally, Webb was inclined to think she hadn't.

The Warrenders lived in a large, mock-Colonial house in several acres of ground. As Jackson drew up in the semicircular drive, there was hysterical barking from a pair of black Labradors fortunately confined behind an ornamental side gate. He had the impression that if loosed, they'd have gone straight for the throat.

They were admitted by a uniformed maid and shown

into the library while "madam" was advised of their arrival.

"Shades of Noël Coward," Webb said, looking about him at the panelled walls.

Jackson grinned. "Isn't this where they were always finding bodies in the good old days?"

Webb grunted. "Unfortunately these days they turn up anywhere."

The door opened and Daphne Warrender came in. She was a heavily corseted woman in her late fifties, carefully made up and wearing a tweed skirt, twin set and pearls. Briefly, Webb wondered if he had indeed wandered on to a stage-set.

"Yes?" she said graciously, the words "my man" hanging unsaid in the air.

Webb, refraining from tugging his forelock, produced his warrant card instead. "I don't know if you've heard, ma'am, about the death of Mr. Neil Carey?"

Her eyelids fluttered. "Yes, I saw a paragraph in *The Times* this morning. A dreadful business."

"I believe you and your husband used to know him?"

"They were business colleagues, yes." She hesitated. "I think, Chief Inspector, my husband would be more help to you than I."

"Indeed, ma'am, if he's at home?"

"He retired last year." She pulled a silken bell-rope and the maid reappeared.

"Ask Mr. Warrender to join us, please, Sarah."

The husband was a tall, lugubrious-looking man with sagging cheeks and a regimental tie. Jackson, recalling Mrs. Carey's comment, conceded that dinner with this pair would hardly be a barrel of laughs.

"Felix, these gentlemen are inquiring about poor Neil."

"I believe he left your firm under some sort of cloud, sir?"

"Very much so. Unfortunate business."

"Could you tell me what it was?"

"Well now, don't like to talk out of turn when the fellow's dead."

"It could be important, sir."

"Very well. I regret to say he was carrying on with my assistant. A most capable young woman she was, too. I'd have thought she had more sense."

"What happened?"

"I came upon them *in flagrante* and all that, in the boardroom. What's more, I had some customers with me at the time. Highly embarrassing."

"I see. So you felt there was nothing for it but to ask for his resignation?"

"Very much so."

"And the woman?"

"Gave in her notice at the same time. All she could do, really."

"What happened to her?"

"Haven't the slightest idea."

"How long ago was all this?"

"Must be over three years now."

Webb turned to Mrs. Warrender, who'd been listening avidly. "You'd be surprised to discover Mr. and Mrs. Carey were still together?"

Her eyes flickered warily. "She mentioned our meeting? Yes, it was a surprise. It hadn't occurred to me she'd stay with him."

"Quite an item of gossip for your friends," he remarked. No response. "I suppose you rang around to tell them?"

"One or two, yes," she answered stiffly.

And they, doubtless, had passed it on, and among those who heard the news might well be someone who was more than interested to learn where Neil Carey was now living. The girl, for instance. If Carey ran true to form, he'd probably not been in touch since.

"I'd be grateful for the names of those you did contact."

"I really don't see—" She broke off, staring at him in

sudden horror. "You surely don't imagine that one of *my friends* killed Neil?"

"No, no," he assured her hastily. "But we need to know who they in turn told. You must admit it's a coincidence that he was killed so soon afterwards."

She seemed prepared to admit no such thing, but her husband broke in.

"Look here, Chief Inspector, fooling around is unfortunately a way of life nowadays. Hardly punishable by death, what?"

"It's a line of inquiry, sir, nothing more. It might well lead nowhere, but it has to be followed through."

While his wife was sulkily giving Jackson the names and addresses of her confidantes, Webb turned back to Warrender.

"What was the young woman called, sir?"

"Mayfield, Belinda Mayfield."

"Was she by any chance married herself?"

"Very much so," Warrender said, for the third time. Whatever happened to the good, old-fashioned word "yes"?

"Do you know where she lived?"

"Afraid not."

"They'd know at the office," Mrs. Warrender put in.

The firm's name and address were also taken down. Someone else could go chasing after this lot, Webb thought feelingly. He'd sit back and wait till they found the girl. Though was it likely, after all this time, that she'd chase after her ex-lover and cut his throat? As he'd admitted to the Warrenders, the whole exercise would probably turn out to be another wild-goose chase.

There was good news of a sort awaiting their return to Carrington Street, late that afternoon. Inquiries into a local shoplifting had brought to light a number of items stolen during the suspected motorway-gang robberies. Crombie and his team already had six or seven other names to work on, and the recovered loot was awaiting identification by its owners, several of whom were now on their way to view it.

But as far as could be seen at the moment, the thieves had no connection whatever either with the graffiti or the murders that followed.

"It's too early to be sure, of course," Crombie told Webb, "but they seem to be professionals, interested only in a quick heist, rapid disposal of the goods and the best possible deal for themselves. If the deaths had occurred on the days of the break-ins it'd be different, but as it is I can't see any link. Sorry, Dave."

"Sod's law," Webb replied. "I couldn't really see it myself either. By the way, when the Parrishes arrive, tell them I'd like to see them, would you. I want a brief word with everyone I've not seen since Carey's death; I'll catch up with the others tomorrow."

"Any particular reason?"

"Just to weigh up previous impressions in the light of the second murder."

It was nearly eight o'clock when the Parrishes were shown into his office, since they couldn't be contacted till they returned from work.

"Well, Chief Inspector!" Parrish said, beaming broadly as he came forward with outstretched hand. "This is the best news we've had in weeks."

"You've recovered some of your possessions?"

"The ones that matter, yes—my wife's jewellery, which was irreplaceable, and several knick-knacks we're fond of. Difficult to get rid of, I suppose, once their descriptions were circulated. No sign of the music centre, but at least it was insured." He gestured to his wife to seat herself, and sat down on the chair opposite Webb. "So what can we do for you?"

"I was wondering, sir, since you live opposite the Lodge, whether you could throw any light on Mr. Carey's death?"

"You mean did we see anything suspicious? I can't say

we did, but it's hardly surprising since we didn't get home till after he'd been found."

"You've been asked about a parked car, I believe?"

"Yes, but I didn't notice it. We're very busy at work just now, so as soon as we get home we draw the curtains, get supper and settle down for the evening." He paused. "It's very disquieting, though, all this sudden violence. Have you any leads?"

"One or two, sir."

"That's good to know. Right, if there's nothing else, then?"

"That's all for the moment, thank you."

Webb watched them go with a jaundiced eye. Any leads, indeed. He'd give his eye-teeth for a good one. He thought back over their previous statements, the most important of which was the overheard quarrel between the Dexters. Why should he feel that was significant? The watch which had caused it had since turned up safely.

And, he reminded himself, Parrish had been in the grounds on Easter Monday. Suppose he and Carol had met, and she'd reminded him about the aerator for her lawn? And then—what?

For a few moments more he pursued his mythical hares. Then with a sigh he abandoned them, realizing that what he was most in need of was hot food and a stiff drink.

Wearily he sorted the papers on his desk into separate piles and put them away. Jackson had gone home long since, eager to check on the boy, who was now making good progress. And Alan was still downstairs interviewing. Good luck to him.

Webb stood up and stretched. After he'd eaten, he told himself, he'd get out his sketching pad. Various niggling impressions were swimming in and out of his memory. With luck they'd sort themselves out when he captured them on paper.

It was peaceful in the little flat at the top of Beechcroft Mansions. Very faintly through the wall came the sound of his neighbour's television, providing a nebulous and unobtrusive companionship. With a couple of pork chops under his belt and a replenished glass of whisky at his side, Webb set himself to the task which usually presented itself at some point in an investigation. Mind maps, the boffins called them, but he'd been doing them long before they'd become fashionable practice. And his facility with cartoons, for which the local paper clamoured ceaselessly, made of his sketches not maps so much as character studies. The little cartoon figures, easily recognizable though with exaggerated features, often pointed him in the way of the villain.

Rapidly he began to draw, beginning with the five households that had attracted the graffiti. A shadowy figure for Carol Dexter, whom he'd seen only in death, with her husband, tall and fair-haired, beside her. The Cummingses, Gina dark and petite, Bob towering over her, and the difficult mother-in-law. Next, Alison and Neil Carey, the flamboyant Parrishes and the retired couple from the bungalow.

For good measure, in the upper corner of the sheet Webb reproduced the grimacing face and studied it for several minutes before continuing with his live cast, the gentle schoolmaster, and the Barlow family: the crippled old man in his wheelchair, the ponderous milkman, the woman in the greenhouse. And their son, as Webb had seen him across the café table. *Had* he known more about the drawings than he'd been prepared to admit?

When he'd peopled the sheet with them all, he sat back and let his eyes move slowly over each one, concentrating as he did so on the statement that person had given, hopeful that one of them might jump forward to claim his attention with some inconsistency. They remained stubbornly static, each in turn staring back at him from the paper, as though daring him to accuse them.

Tearing off the sheet, he let it fall to the floor and began on the scene of crime, drawing the village of Beckworth in cartographical detail, houses, pub, forest, and the spreading gardens of its Stately Home—the path which led to the lily-pond and the pool itself, encrusted with lily-pads.

Now came the crucial part, the merging of people and places. On the second sheet he began to insert little figures in the positions where they claimed to have been when first Carol Dexter, then (in different coloured crayon) Neil Carey, had met their deaths. And over this sheet he sat long and silently, from time to time reaching out a hand to his whisky glass but barely registering the fiery liquid as it went down his throat.

Could Neil Carey's past, known now to have been peppered with affairs, have any bearing on his meeting with Carol Dexter? Suppose they *had* arranged to meet on the Monday, while Dexter was taking the children to his sister? Suppose that in the seclusion of the herbaceous border he had made advances to her, confident they'd be acceptable. And if they hadn't? If she'd drawn back, perhaps flared out at him? Might he have hit her, knocking her over to bang her head on the metal urn they'd found covered in her blood?

And again and again he came back to the fact that of the five recipients of the graffiti, she alone had been alarmed by it. Why? Had some deep-buried instinct warned her that it foreshadowed her death? If so, the same instinct had not served Neil Carey, who'd dismissed the drawing out of hand. Yet it was oddly disturbing that those two, both of whom had disliked the village, had both died there.

Webb rubbed his hands over his eyes and looked at his watch. It was well past midnight and he was suddenly desperately tired. Tomorrow, he would see the live counterparts of some of these drawings, and perhaps after that things would fall into place.

Leaving the paper on the easel, he turned out the light and went to bed.

## CHAPTER 13

Webb's habit of sketching people and places in a case was well known at Carrington Street, and regarded with almost superstitious awe since it so frequently bore results. They referred to it among themselves as "the Governor 'drawing conclusions'."

The next morning on the drive to Beckworth, Jackson deduced, from Webb's continuing abstraction, that he had been at work the previous night.

"Any new ideas to kick around, Guv?" he ventured, to break the long silence.

Webb stirred and his eyes focused. "Only that it seems we have two cases in one. Different motives, different murderers."

"Great!" Jackson muttered under his breath. Then, curiously, "But there *were* links between the victims even apart from them living in the same place. The car-ride, the graffiti—"

"True. But the more I think about it, the more convinced I am that Carol Dexter's death was an accident."

"You mean," Jackson asked sarcastically, "her murderer thought that even though she was unconscious, she could still swim?"

"No," Webb said patiently, "the accident was in her cracking her head. And when she lay there motionless he thought he'd killed her, panicked, and tried to hide her body."

Jackson thought it over. "But you're sure it wasn't Carey?"

"By no means. It could well have been."

"But even if it was, you reckon his death was unconnected with hers?"

"Yep."

Jackson sighed. "Well, I hope it all makes more sense to you than it does to me."

To which Webb made no reply.

Their first call was at the Scotts' portion of the schoolhouse. Mrs. Scott came to the door, her neat grey jumper and skirt matching her hair. She smiled a welcome.

"Come in, Chief Inspector; you've saved my husband a walk. He was wondering how to contact you."

"Oh? Has something come up?"

"Perhaps he should tell you himself." She pushed open the living-room door, raising her voice slightly. "Leslie, the police are here."

"Ah, Chief Inspector! Good to see you! I was going to leave a message for you at the village hall. I presume your men are still there?"

"Yes, and likely to be for some time now we've a second murder."

"Alas, yes. Well, what I wanted to say to you is this: one of your chaps was round the other day asking about cars parked across the road. I said I hadn't seen one, but . . ." He gave a little shrug and smiled ruefully. "My memory isn't what it was, I'm afraid. Last night as I lay in bed turning things over in my mind, I remembered that I had indeed seen a car I didn't recognize last week, though it wasn't parked. That was probably why I didn't think of it."

"You mean you saw it arrive?"

"Exactly that. I was in here one evening—I'm almost sure it was Wednesday—when there was a sudden outburst of barking outside. We've had a spot of bother with the paper-boy leaving the gate open, so I went to the window to see if the dogs had got into the garden. They hadn't, but sure enough the gate was open, so I went out to close it. And as I was doing so Mr. Carey drove up the road. He turned into Tinker's Lane and drove round behind the Green Man, where he garages his car. Used to garage it, that is.

"The dogs were still circling each other on the pavement, growling and jumping about, and I was trying to remember who they belonged to, because if they became excited and ran into the road it could have been dangerous. And while I was watching them, this other car came quickly along the road and also turned into Tinker's Lane. Then it suddenly stopped, and I remember wondering if the driver was looking for Mr. Carey. At that point he reappeared on foot round the corner of the Green Man, crossed the road in front of the stationary car, and went through the little gate into the grounds. I remember he waved to me as he did so."

"And what did the other car do?"

"Alas, there I must disappoint you. After returning Mr. Carey's wave I came back into the house. I've no idea where it went."

"Did you get a good look at the driver?"

"Not really. It was getting dark, and he was going quite fast as he rounded the corner, as though he expected Mr. Carey's car to be some way ahead of him."

"It was a man, anyway?"

"Oh yes, no doubt about that. But whether young or old, fair or dark, fat or thin, I haven't the remotest idea. I'm so sorry."

"This idea that he was looking for Mr. Carey's car; is that with the benefit of hindsight?"

"No," the old man said consideringly, "it was the way it struck me at the time."

"And you think it likely he turned into the estate carpark?"

"To be honest, Chief Inspector, I didn't give it another thought. But if he wanted to see Mr. Carey, then yes, I suppose he might have done." He paused. *"Did* he call at the Lodge?"

"Not as far as we know." Webb turned to Jackson. "Can you check, Sergeant, when Mrs. Carey saw the car?"

They all waited while Jackson flicked through the pages

of his notebook. "Wednesday 29th was the first occasion, sir. As she was going to bed."

"Then it tallies!" Scott said excitedly.

"What time did you see it?"

"It was just before supper, I remember. About half past six."

"And you didn't see it again?"

"I'm afraid not."

"Do you ever go over to the pub, sir?"

"Only very rarely these days. Not for several months now." He paused, then said eagerly, "Have I been any help?"

"I think you might well have been. It seems likely Mr. Carey was followed home, and it's certainly possible that has some bearing on his death."

"Well, that's gratifying. Thank goodness I told you about it." He hesitated. "Chief Inspector, on your last visit I was telling you about Darren Barlow. Did you interview him?"

"Yes, we did." Meeting the old man's anxious eyes, he added, "I don't think he'd anything to do with all this."

Scott sat back in his chair. "I can't tell you how relieved I am. I felt very badly afterwards about having mentioned him, but at the time it seemed my civic duty."

As before, the detectives went from the Scotts' house to the Barlows'. Though Webb had seen Mrs. Barlow and her daughter two days previously, he had not spoken to the men of the house since Carey's death.

Joe Barlow had just returned from his milk round and was sitting at the kitchen table with a mug of tea. Webb was struck by his pallor; it seemed he hadn't shaken off his virus after all. He looked up dully as his wife showed them into the room.

"We're checking to see if anyone noticed anything which could shed a light on Mr. Carey's death," Webb said lightly, hoping to put him at his ease.

Barlow shook his head.

"It's really shaken Joe, has that," Hazel volunteered. "He's been off his food ever since he heard."

"He was a friend of yours?" Knowing the infrastructure of village life, it didn't seem likely.

"I hardly knew him," Joe said expressionlessly. "Hazel sees a lot of his wife, though, what with the flowers and all."

"But if you hardly knew him," Webb persisted gently, "why has his death upset you so much?"

His wife answered for him. "Because he's the second person in a week to be killed here! Isn't that enough to upset anyone?"

"Mr. Barlow?"

"Like the wife says. To think there's someone going round who'd do a thing like that." His hand shook suddenly and he put the mug down.

"It must be a madman," his wife said. "That's the only explanation."

"Do you go to the Green Man, Mr. Barlow?"

"What?" Barlow wrenched his attention back.

"The pub. Do you often go there?"

"Wednesdays and Saturdays, most weeks."

Webb felt Jackson's heightened interest. "Was there anyone there last Wednesday you hadn't seen before?"

"Not as I recall."

"Would you have noticed if there had been?"

"Yes, I reckon so. I was sitting at the bar all evening."

Another promising lead dried up. Webb turned to the woman. "You haven't by any chance seen any strangers about? Hanging round outside Beckworth Lodge, for instance?"

She shook her head. "No, sir."

Webb stifled a sigh. "Very well. Thank you." He got to his feet. "We'd like to see Mr. Barlow senior before we go."

The front room was warm and stuffy but the old man had a rug over his knees. He was watching television, a disgruntled expression on his face.

"You again!" he greeted them. "What is it this time? Not much good at stopping folk being murdered, are you?"

"We're doing our best," Webb said mildly. "Did you know Mr. Carey?"

"He sometimes stopped for a word when I was on the gate. Pleasant enough, for an incomer."

"Know anyone who had it in for him?"

The old man shook his head. "Couldn't be anyone local, 'less it was that man whose wife was killed."

"Why do you say that?"

"Well, one thing leads to another, doesn't it?"

Which enigmatic comment was the most he was prepared to offer.

They lunched at the Green Man, where Webb repeated his question about strangers and received the same reply. If the car Scott saw was the one Mrs. Carey'd noticed, it seemed the driver'd sat alone in it for five hours or more. Unless, of course, he'd visited Carey at the Lodge without his wife's knowledge. Or anyone else in Beckworth, come to that. Another round of questioning to be done.

At the incident room, however, there was more positive news.

"DS Partridge just phoned in, sir. He left a number and would like you to ring back."

Webb went into the small back room, which was presumably used for Sunday School; there was a lumpy Easter Garden on a shelf, and highly coloured drawings of improbable donkeys round the walls.

"DS Partridge."

"Hello, Don. I believe you called."

"Yes, Guv." Partridge's voice quickened into animation. "We've traced the girl who was involved with Carey, and guess what—she's dead, too!"

"Must be catching. Recently?"

"No, over two years ago. In childbirth, apparently."

"And her husband?"

"He works on an offshore oil rig, but he's on leave at

the moment. We haven't seen him; I thought you might like to go yourself."

"I would indeed." Webb fumbled for notebook and pen. "What's his address?"

"Pinner. Fourteen Linden Avenue."

"OK, Don, thanks."

He went back to the incident room, where Jackson was watching one of the computer screens. "M4 again for us, old son. Husband of Carey's deceased lady-friend."

"Deceased? Then she didn't do it."

"No, but he might have. She died in childbirth two years ago. Could have been Carey's."

"Would the husband have known?"

"Quite likely. He works on an oil rig, and if he wasn't home at the appropriate time . . ." Webb lifted his shoulders expressively.

"But what has all this to do with Mrs. Dexter?" Jackson asked, as they went out to the car.

"I keep telling you, Ken, damn-all." And he opened the door and climbed inside.

Linden Avenue had seen better days. Some of the houses had been turned into flats, and several front gardens were concreted over to provide parking space. There was a general run-down air about it, though one or two houses were defiantly double-glazed.

Number 14 was a small semi at the far end, and there was a car in the drive. So far, so good. As Jackson drew in to the kerb, Webb glanced up and saw a face at the downstairs window before it darted back out of sight. However, their knock was answered, and they found themselves facing a large, broad-shouldered man with curly ginger hair. He was wearing an open-necked shirt and jeans.

"Mr. Mayfield?"

"That's right."

"Chief Inspector Webb and Sergeant Jackson, from Shillingham."

"Where?"

"Shillingham, sir. Broadshire."

"Yes?"

"Could we come inside? We have a few questions to ask you."

"What kind of questions?" It wasn't said aggressively. In fact, there was as little expression in his voice as in the pale blue eyes that steadily returned Webb's gaze.

"Concerning the death of Mr. Neil Carey."

"The one in the paper? What's it to do with me?"

"We believe your late wife was a friend of his."

For a moment longer Mayfield maintained his stance. Then his shoulders sagged. "All right. You'd better come in."

The hall felt cold and unlived-in and there were boxes and packing cases against the wall.

"You'll have to forgive the mess," Mayfield said over his shoulder. "I'm hardly ever here."

He led them, probably instinctively, to the kitchen. It was long and narrow, and at the far end was a drop table and two chairs. These he indicated, and as they sat down, drew up a stool for himself. Through the pane in the back door Webb could see a paved area and a small square of neglected garden.

"Now, what's all this about?"

Webb said, "We were sorry to hear of your wife's death."

Mayfield's fingers clenched, but he said steadily, "That was some time ago now."

"What happened to the child?"

"It died too."

"That's tough." He paused. "I believe you work on an oil rig, Mr. Mayfield?"

"Been doing your homework, haven't you?"

"Away for long stretches at a time, are you?"

There was silence. Then Mayfield said softly, "Damn you."

"Look, sir, this isn't easy, with your wife being dead and everything."

"But was the child mine? That's what you're getting at, isn't it? Well, it wasn't, it was that bastard Carey's."

"She told you?"

"Yes, she told me. And you know something? I agreed to accept it. You see, it wasn't only because I'd been away that I knew it wasn't mine. I can't father kids myself. Belinda'd always wanted one, and we'd talked round adoption, but I wasn't keen. You don't know what you're getting. At least this one would have been half hers."

"Wouldn't you have resented it, though?"

He shrugged. "Never got the chance to find out. The poor little blighter was premature and died within hours. Belinda was haemorrhaging badly and needed a transfusion." He stopped, then ended flatly, "She was given contaminated blood. She didn't stand a chance."

There was a silence. Pointless to keep saying they were sorry. He knew it anyway. Webb said, "And you blamed Neil Carey."

"Too right I did. If it hadn't been for him, she wouldn't have died. But by that time he'd gone off God knows where, and in any case he was the last person I wanted to see. I went back to the rig and worked all the hours God sent. I told myself it would get easier; after all, we were used to being apart. But she'd always been here at home, waiting. The Carey business hadn't been serious; we both knew that. He set his cap at her and she was lonely. A lot of blokes in our profession run up against that. With what we had going between us, we could have coped. But we didn't get the chance."

He stared down at his clenched hands. "Everyone said it would get easier, but it hasn't. Each time I come back here, I expect to find her. Daft, isn't it? People tell me I should sell, move out, but how can I? It was our home. It's all I have left of her."

"And then," Webb said heavily, "by chance you learned where Carey was."

"Yes. From a chap at Stanley Marcus. We used to go to the pub sometimes with him and his wife. He heard on the grapevine that Carey had a job with Banks Moorhouse in Reading.

"Well, I was on leave and I'd nothing else to do. I went along out of curiosity, to see what the man who'd wrecked my life looked like. I was going to ask someone to point him out to me, but it wasn't necessary. There was a car-park at the back of the building, and as luck would have it, the directors had their own spaces with their names printed on a board. I only had to wait till five o'clock, and when he came out and got into that car, I'd know who he was. Honest to God, that's all I meant to do—have a look at him.

"But when he did come there was a pretty girl with him, and they were laughing and joking together. And I thought, 'What if he's got his eye on her, and she's happily married? Will some other poor bastard have to go through this?' "

"Mr. Mayfield," Webb interrupted, "I think we should caution you that—"

"Save your breath. You want to hear this, don't you, and I don't give a damn any more."

"Nevertheless . . ." Webb nodded to Jackson, who obliged. Mayfield waited impatiently till he'd finished, then immediately continued.

"Anyway, the girl went off to her car and I watched Carey get into his. And without even thinking about it I started to follow him. I never even wondered where he was going; he could have driven to Scotland for all I cared, I'd still have stuck on his tail. But he went to this place up on the hill in your part of the world.

"Well, as you know, there's a pub opposite where he lived, and it seemed quite likely he'd come over for a pint later on. I didn't want to go to his house, because his wife

mightn't know about Belinda. So I sat and waited till closing time, but he didn't come so I drove home.

"The next day I went back to Reading and waited for
him again. By this time it had got to me. All I could think
of was the way he'd laughed and chatted with that girl,
while Belinda would never laugh again. She'd paid with her
life for the time they spent together, but he'd got off scot-
free. I could feel the hatred building up in me. I knew I
should stop then, let it go, but I couldn't.

"Well, the same thing happened again. He went home
and stayed there. Who could blame him, with a wife waiting? If I wanted to approach him, it seemed it would have
to be before he got there. Over the weekend I worked out
what I'd do, planned it down to the smallest detail. It was
the most exhilarating two days I can remember; for the first
time in two years my life had some purpose to it. And on
Monday, I went ahead of him to the woods halfway up the
hill. I parked my car there, then I walked back to the main
road and waited for him at the turning. I'd allowed plenty
of time, and it was just as well, because he was early. And
when he arrived, I hitched a lift up the hill."

Outside, an aeroplane droned over a cloudless blue sky.
Inside there was silence. Then Mayfield looked up. "Well,
you can probably guess the rest. I'd taken a knife with me
and I forced him to park next to my car in the lay-by,
screening it from the road. Then I made him walk with me
into the forest. And I told him who I was, and exactly what
had happened to Belinda. He insisted he hadn't known she
was pregnant. It might have been true. On the other hand,
he'd have said anything at that moment."

He sighed and looked up at Webb. "So there you have
it. I didn't think it'd take long to find me."

Damn that Warrender woman! Webb thought vehe-
mently. If it hadn't been for her gossiping phone calls,
Carey would be alive and this man guilt-free.

Mayfield had got to his feet, lion-like with his broad
shoulders and red mane. He must have been a terrifying

figure in the dim forest, with the knife in his hand. Well, Neil Carey hadn't got off scot-free after all; he'd paid the same price as Belinda Mayfield.

# CHAPTER 14

Murder on Monday, arrest on Thursday had a ring of "Solomon Grundy" about it. It didn't usually happen so swiftly, and Webb wished he could feel duly gratified; instead, he felt profoundly depressed. In part this was due to his sympathy for their prisoner, but also because, as he'd suspected, finding the answer to one crime had brought them no nearer to solving the other.

Before going to work the next morning, he stood for some moments staring at his sketches. The murderer was depicted here, he was sure of it. In his mind's eye he moved the little figures about in a deadly gavotte. If this one had been *here* instead of there, could he—? But why?

At Carrington Street he brushed aside Crombie's congratulations. "It was handed to me on a plate," he said.

"Good PR none the less. And there's something else to celebrate; Regional Crime have collared another four of the motorway gang. What's more, once they knew they were nailed two of them admitted seeing the graffiti at Mews Grange."

Webb looked up. "What day would that have been?"

Crombie consulted his notes. "They turned it over on the Tuesday, and the drawing was there then. The day before the Dexters got theirs."

Webb said irritably, "It's perfectly ridiculous that we can't discover who did it. Damn it, *someone* must have seen something."

"Not necessarily. Those high hedges shield the houses from the road."

Webb stood up with a sigh. "Well, I'd better go and tell Mrs. Carey we've nabbed the bloke who did for her old man."

"Good luck!" Crombie said, and bent once more over his files.

It was a cold and sunny morning. Primroses were scattered over the grass, daffodils nodded and purple aubretia cascaded over stone walls. In Chantock Forest the trees were washed with soft green and the sunlight filtered through the branches to make checkered patterns on the road. *Where every prospect pleases,* Webb thought glumly, *And only man is vile.* And he averted his eyes from the lay-by where Carey's car had been found.

"I need some space to think, Ken," he told Jackson as they entered the village. "You go and break the news to Mrs. Carey. And you might let the Cummings know, too; they'll be going back to London tomorrow."

"Wonder if they'll ever come back?" Jackson mused. "I don't think I would, in their shoes."

Webb got out of the car. "See you in a couple of hours at the incident room."

The village appeared deserted. News of the arrest had reached the incident room the previous evening, and inquiries about the second murder were thankfully abandoned. With police presence chiefly confined to the village hall, Beckworth had sunk back into the daytime lethargy which had so depressed Carol Dexter.

Thinking of her, Webb walked back along the main road and stood on the pavement outside the bungalows, staring across at her home. The house itself had figured largely in the tragedy. Its front door had been daubed, it had been the scene of the quarrel which the Parrishes overheard, and from it Carol had gone to meet her death. *Why* had she been killed? Had he been wrong to attach so much importance to the graffiti? They'd been shown to have no connection with either Neil Carey's death or the burglaries.

Perhaps they also had no bearing on hers. Yet of all those who'd been subjected to the drawing, she alone had been disturbed by it—and within a week she was dead.

His eyes moved from the glowing stone farmhouse to the building that had been its stables, now itself upgraded to a desirable residence. How had they both looked when the Barlows lived there, when there had been a school and a shop and a bit of heart in the village? He would never know.

He turned and walked slowly back along the road, stopping at the crossroads to look reflectively at the winding drive of Beckworth House visible through its gates. Mentally he followed Carol along the length of it to the forecourt in front of the House. Gina Cummings had seen her there. Where had she gone next? Directly to the lily-pond? And who had seen her go?

Within the gates the small stone lodge lay humped in the sunshine. Jackson would be there with Mrs. Carey. Would it help her to know how and why her husband had died?

Webb turned into Tinker's Lane, still sifting the pros and cons of the case, but his musings were interrupted by a sudden scuffle in one of the gardens, and he turned to see a large black cat erupt from the shelter of some shrubbery in pursuit of a bird. With millimetres to spare, the bird soared to freedom, and Webb watched it alight on the faded swinging sign outside the pub, chattering nervously.

He was about to start walking again when his eyes slipped to the sign itself and he stiffened unbelievingly. For beneath the bird-droppings, the flaking paint and the weathering of many years, there was, faintly discernible, the outline of a face. Its features were no longer visible, but twisting branches of leaves sprang from its head and Webb knew without doubt that it had once had squinting eyes, a protruding tongue and a malevolent expression. For it was the Green Man, one of the ancient gods, the spirit of the countryside. And all the time it had been swinging secretively above their heads, no doubt mocking their endeavours.

He pushed his way through the swing doors into the pub. The proprietor straightened from behind the bar. "Sorry, sir, we're not open. Oh, it's you."

"That sign of yours, Mr. Haydock. I've never noticed it before."

"Oh?" The man waited, puzzled. Then he said, "I suppose people don't look up there. The name's written on the wall, anyway."

"And if they did look up, they'd have difficulty making out what it was."

"Yes, you're right there. We keep meaning to take it down and get it repainted."

"Other pubs called the Green Man depict Robin Hood in his Lincoln green."

"Yes, well that's a more modern interpretation," said the landlord, dismissing with magnificent nonchalance an eight-hundred-year-old legend. "Ours is the original one. Ugly little chap, isn't he?"

Webb drew a deep breath. The ancient spirit of the countryside, deeply resentful of the newcomers usurping village homes. And those newcomers who'd been visited by it had none of them been here longer than three years. They wouldn't have recognized the drawing as the faded, indecipherable inn sign swinging in the lane.

Webb turned on his heel and pushed his way out again, leaving the landlord staring after him.

Mrs. Barlow greeted his appearance with a sigh of resignation. "This is becoming quite a habit," she said.

"Unavoidable, I'm afraid."

He followed her down the passage, aware of Bert Barlow's bright, rheumy eyes staring at him as he passed his open door. Joe was at the sink rinsing his tea mug. He turned sharply as Webb came into the room, and a flicker of fear crossed his face.

"Mr. Barlow, I think you're aware we've been asking about the graffiti which appeared on five doors in the village?"

"Aye, I heard."

"And you disclaimed all knowledge of it?"

"Well, of course he did," Hazel said indignantly. "So did we all."

Webb kept his eyes on her husband. "But weren't you in fact responsible, sir?"

Hazel gasped and turned to Joe, waiting for him to deny it. He stood stock still, staring back at Webb.

"Didn't you draw a Green Man on the doors of the incomers, to show your resentment of their taking over village homes?"

"I might have done," he said at last.

"Joe!"

"There was no harm in it," he said defensively.

"I suppose you did it on your early morning rounds, when no one was about? And if anyone did see you coming back down a drive they'd think nothing of it. You're the milkman, after all."

"Oh, Joe!" Hazel said reproachfully.

"Why the Lodge, though? That's hardly a village house, and the Careys aren't keeping anyone else out."

Barlow was silent, but his wife said hesitantly, "I applied for that job, before they came. I thought if me and Joe could move out, there'd be more room here for the others."

The last piece of the jigsaw. Webb leant against the Welsh dresser, his arms folded. "You say there was no harm done, and I agree that to most of them the scribbles were simply a nuisance; as, I imagine, you intended them to be. But Mrs. Dexter was really frightened by it. And she died a few days later."

The silence in the room was total.

"The most terrible thing about her death," Webb went on deliberately, "was that it was almost certainly unnecessary."

"How d'you mean?" Hazel whispered.

"We think what happened was an accident. For some reason she fell—she was pushed, hit, something like that. She cracked her head on an urn—we found blood on it— and was knocked unconscious. We think the person she was with tried to rouse her, and when he couldn't, he thought she was dead. So he panicked, and in an attempt to conceal her body, threw her in the pond. But in fact it wasn't the bang on the head that killed her; she drowned."

Hazel was staring at him in horror. "Oh no!"

Joe Barlow made a low, anguished sound in his throat. Then he swung round to the sink, gripping it with both hands, his body arched over it as though he were about to vomit.

"Joe!" His wife flew to him, gripping his arm. "What is it? Are you ill?" She turned her wild face to Webb. "Get help—quickly!"

"It's not medical help he needs, Mrs. Barlow."

She hadn't heard him, still focused entirely on her husband. "What is it, love? Are you in pain? Come and sit down and we'll get the doctor."

His great shoulders were heaving, but no sound came from him. Webb, hating every minute, bided his time. Then very slowly, Joe turned. His face was a sickly yellow and the eyes which stared from it raw with agony.

Webb said gently, "Your wife's right, Mr. Barlow, you should sit down."

"Is that true, what you just said?" The words seemed torn out of him. "She drowned? You're not just trying to trick me?"

"Joe!" Hazel, now as white as her husband, clutched at him again. "You don't know what you're saying! Hush now!" He shook her off, waiting for Webb's reply.

"She drowned," he confirmed.

Joe jerked his head distractedly, as though plagued by a swarm of wasps. But he allowed his wife to lead him to the table, where he collapsed into a chair and leant forward, his head buried in his arms.

Hazel hurried to the dresser for a glass and filled it at the sink. "You mustn't listen to him," she told Webb urgently, as she tried to offer the water to Joe. "He doesn't know what he's saying."

"I think he does, Mrs. Barlow, and I think we must let him say it. But first I have to caution him." Joe raised his haggard face. "You understand what that means?" He nodded. "All right, then, go on."

Barlow moistened his lips, but he did not speak. In the brief silence Webb heard the soft swish of wheels in the passage, and knew that, just out of sight, the old man was sitting listening. So be it. Everyone would know soon enough.

"Come along, Mr. Barlow," he prompted, "let's get it over. When we spoke before, you made it very clear you didn't like Mrs. Dexter, though you didn't say she was living in your old home."

"That wasn't her fault!" Hazel interrupted. "Joe didn't blame her personally. He even helped out in the garden."

"And changed fuses for her," Webb said, his eyes on the man at the table.

"You caught on to that, then," Barlow said dully.

Hazel looked from one to the other in bewilderment. "What's so special about fuses?"

"He was alone upstairs for a while, and later Mr. Dexter couldn't find his watch."

She said furiously, "I hope you're not suggesting Joe took it?"

"No, I am suggesting he was *accused* of taking it. It was quite simply the last straw, wasn't it?"

Joe slowly let his breath out, his large body slumping.

"Suppose you tell us what happened?"

"Since you know so much," the man said dully, "you might as well hear the rest." He reached for the glass and drained its contents in one draught. His wife had lowered herself into the chair next to him, silent and afraid.

"Our family'd lived at Coppins for generations," he began, speaking slowly and stopping every now and then to search for the right words. "We thought we'd always be there. But then Dad had his accident, I wasn't old enough to run the farm, and we had to get out. The day we left was, right up till last week, the most terrible of my life."

Hazel said softly, "You never said."

"Well, there was no sense in going on about it. Fretting wouldn't put things right. But that day, with the cart standing loaded with all our belongings, I made a solemn vow. One day we'd go back."

There was a brief pause and his audience, including the unseen listener in the passage, waited for him to continue.

"I'd expected to get a job with George Powell, who took over Coppins. I wasn't afraid of work and I knew the land. But he'd three sons of his own, and there was no work for me. I tried the other farms round about but they'd nothing either, so, as we needed the money, I went to the dairy. But I missed the land and I talked the head gardener up at the House into letting me help out part-time. And I went on hoping and planning. It kept me going when things were hard."

Hazel fished in her apron pocket for a handkerchief and blew her nose. "I never realized," she whispered.

"I was a fool, I see that now. We've had a good life together and there are plenty worse off. But I was always hankering after Coppins, for Dad's sake as well as mine, and the waiting was eating away at me. Then old man Powell died and his sons left the farm to work in machinery. It was the chance I'd been waiting for. I went straight to his Grace and asked to go back. I couldn't see there'd be any objection; we were former tenants and he knew our standards."

He paused, remembering. "But he told me he'd decided to sell off Coppins and its land to developers. It was—well

—a bombshell. I just couldn't believe it. He was embarrassed, I could see that, and quite apologetic, but nothing I could say would change his mind. Anyway"—he moved impatiently—"to cut a long story short, the builders moved in, the stables were converted and other houses went up in the fields we used to plough. But still, pig-headed as I was, I wouldn't accept I'd never get back there. Not till Mrs. Dexter asked me to fix her plug.

"You see, she showed me all over the house. To be fair, she didn't know I'd been in it before—and I might as well not have been, because there was hardly a part of it I recognized. Everything I remembered had gone, and it was just like something in the glossy magazines.

"I didn't say a word and she must have thought I was impressed, because she said, 'The previous owners wouldn't recognize it, would they?' As though it was something to be *proud* of. Then she said, 'I don't know how long we'll stay, but the price will have doubled by the time we sell.' Can you believe it? After destroying the place, they didn't even intend to settle there! It was just a means of making money.

"The room where the fuse had blown was the one we'd all been born in, me and Dad and Grandad, and who knows how many before him. Not a few of them died there, too. And you should see it now—all gold and white like a wedding cake, with mirrors and frilly curtains."

He lapsed into silence, staring down at the worn surface of the table. Eventually Webb prompted him.

"What happened on Easter Monday?"

Barlow drew a deep breath, but his voice had steadied now. "When I got back from work Darren and his pals were here, playing loud music and drinking. I asked him to turn it down, but he gave me lip."

He spread his hands helplessly. "All I wanted was to change into my slippers and sit down with the paper, but there was nowhere to go. Hazel and Mavis were at the House serving teas, so I thought I might as well go and do some gardening, in the hope it would calm me down. I was in a fair old state by then, because the row with Darren was part of the same old worry about lack of space and Mavis and the baby and all, and I just didn't see how we could cope. I remembered reading somewhere that rats which are kept in a confined space turn killer. And that was when I really hit rock bottom and faced the fact that I'd nothing to strive for any more. After all these years there was no point in trying to go back to Coppins, because the place I'd known no longer existed. That stupid woman and her family had destroyed it.

"Well, I went to get my tools, hoping some hard digging would get it all out of my system. But as luck would have it she was there. She caught sight of me and came hurrying after."

That had been a flaw in his reasoning, Webb thought; he'd assumed Carol's killer had tracked her down. In fact, it was she who'd followed him.

"She was quite the last person I wanted to see just then," Joe was continuing. "And she started on about her husband's watch, and how it had been on the tallboy in the bedroom and now they couldn't find it. And it suddenly dawned on me she was hinting I might have taken it. Me, who'd never touched a penny that wasn't mine."

The kitchen clock ticked, but for several long minutes there was no other sound. Then Joe said dully, "As God's my witness I didn't mean to hurt her. But something just— exploded inside and I lashed out—against fate as much as her—and caught her on the side of her face. She staggered backwards, lost her footing, and went crashing to the ground."

He stared down at the table while his audience waited, scarcely breathing. "Well, I was horrified at what I'd done and hurried to help her up. But she just lay there, not moving. I knelt beside her and lifted her head, and then I saw the blood—a lot of it—and the great gash in her head. I was certain I'd killed her."

Hazel started to cry quietly. The old man, unnoticed, had silently wheeled himself forward until he sat in full view in the open doorway. He looked stunned, an unhappy old ghost.

"I panicked, like you said. I pulled off her watch and took the money from her bag to make it look like a mugging. Then I realized I couldn't just leave her there, so I— well, you know what I did. But I've got the watch and money safe; I was trying to think of a way of getting them to her husband."

No one spoke. Joe raised his head and looked at all of them in turn, ending with Webb. "And now," he concluded flatly, "you tell me she wasn't dead at all, and if I'd gone and got help she'd have recovered."

Suddenly the old man propelled himself forward. "But he never meant nothing!" he cried. "It wasn't murder!"

Webb said quietly, "Nevertheless, sir, that's what he'll be charged with. But I'm sure a good case will be made for reducing it to manslaughter."

Leaving the room, he walked quickly back up the passage, opened the front door and looked outside. A couple of uniformed men were passing the gate.

"Get back to the incident room at the double, will you. Tell Sergeant Jackson to come straight down here with the car."

"Yes, sir." Startled, the two men began to run up the hill, and Webb, bracing himself to face the three stricken people in the kitchen, went back to wait for Jackson.

"So there you have it," Webb said to Hannah a couple of evenings later, "end of both cases. And it's thanks to you that we tracked Mayfield down so quickly."

"You don't sound very happy about it," Hannah remarked astutely, passing him some steak pie.

"No. Why can't villains be thoroughly nasty blokes it'd be a pleasure to collar? Ninety percent are pretty ordinary, but it's a long time since I've had as much sympathy as I have for these two. They were just mild, decent men who had both, in their separate ways, been driven beyond endurance."

"What put you on to Barlow?" Hannah asked curiously.

"A lot of little things just came together. He was the slow, quiet type who bottles things up till they suddenly boil over. That struck me when I was sketching him; it's a type I've come across before in murder cases. And I knew he'd been under strain: cramped living conditions, worry about his son, who couldn't get a job locally and had got into bad company.

"I also knew he hadn't liked Carol Dexter, but I only found out later he used to live at Coppins himself. Then there was the quarrel about the watch. Carol had been upset, knowing her husband was still angry about it. Suppose she'd suddenly caught sight of Barlow—who'd said quite openly he was in the grounds that day—and decided to have it out with him, hoping, perhaps, to get the watch back without any more trouble?"

He sipped his wine. "And having got that far, his upset after her death assumed significance. The doctor wrote it off as a virus, but it was more likely delayed shock. Then he over-reacted to Carey's death—afraid, I imagine, that his action had somehow triggered off another killing.

"But it was the Green Man that clinched it. Of the principal people in the case, only Joe Barlow had lived there long enough to remember the original appearance of the pub sign. And though we hadn't appreciated it, he had a deep-rooted grudge against the wealthy newcomers. In fact, the retired couple had actually bought the bungalow his daughter was after before the developers got their hands on it. But one good thing's come out of all this; I heard today that the Duke has offered the young couple a cottage on the estate."

"A pity he didn't do it sooner. OK, so you sussed Barlow for the graffiti, but they'd no connection with the murders, had they?"

"Certainly not with Carey's. Come to that, the drawing on the Dexters' door wasn't meant as a threat either—just a reaction to seeing over the house the previous day. Probably Carol's general unhappiness exaggerated her fears. Yet I felt all along it was linked with her death, and there's no denying the hand which drew that face on her door was the hand that killed her."

Hannah shuddered. "What'll happen to him?"

"It's my bet they'll go for diminished responsibility, which undoubtedly it was. The charge will almost certainly be manslaughter, but I shouldn't be surprised, when all the facts are known, if he's found Not Guilty."

"Let's hope so. And Mayfield?"

"A different kettle of fish, I'm afraid. Whatever the provocation, that murder was premeditated. Only a plea of insanity could save him, and I doubt if they'll go for that. Still, he's created his own prison over the last two years, and I doubt if an outer one will make much difference. He'll cope.

"It's odd, you know: both men were driven to their limits by the attitudes prevailing today. Carey's sexual 'grab what you can' creed pushed Mayfield over the edge, and the Duke's eye for the main chance did for old Barlow."

He grinned. "Sorry, love. You know I often wax philosophical at this stage. All the same, it strikes me that in both these cases the murderers were victims too. The real culprit was greed."

"In which case," said Hannah, straight-faced, "I'd better not offer you another piece of pie."

*About the Author*

Anthea Fraser was making up stories and poems before she could write, and stated at the age of five that her ambition in life was to be an author. She began writing professionally when her two daughters were small.

Her first publications were short stories (to which, between novels, she has recently returned) and her first novel was published in 1970. Since then she has had twenty-five accepted, including romantic fiction, stories of the paranormal and, latterly, crime. Her work has been translated into seven languages. *Symbols at Your Door* is her seventh novel for the Crime Club.

Anthea Fraser has been Secretary of the Crime Writers' Association since 1986.